T0195909

POISON AND ANTIDOTE

BOHEMIAN STORIES

LEE FOUST

authorHOUSE®

AuthorHouse™
1663 Liberty Drive
Bloomington, IN 47403
www.authorhouse.com
Phone: 1 (800) 839-8640

This is a work of fiction. All of the characters, names, incidents, organizations, and dialogue in this novel are either the products of the author's imagination or are used fictitiously.

Published by AuthorHouse 06/26/2015

ISBN: 978-1-4969-4565-5 (sc)
ISBN: 978-1-4969-4564-8 (hc)
ISBN: 978-1-4969-4563-1 (e)

Library of Congress Control Number: 2014918004

Print information available on the last page.

This book is printed on acid-free paper.

CONTENTS

ACKNOWLEDGMENTS

"Growing Up" appeared in David S. Wills's online journal *Fuck Fiction* and in Paul Corman-Roberts's quarterly fiction section of *Full of Crow*. The "Seventh Street" portion of "Devin Wants to Make a Movie" was published, in both written and aural forms, in LeRoy Chatfield's online *Syndic Literary Journal*. The "A Setting" section of the same story showed up in Laura Eley and Lorna London's *Origami Journal*. The complete story was published in Kerri Farrell Foley's online *Crack the Spine Literary Magazine*. "The Morning of the Day" can be both read and heard online at Sydney, Australia's *Vending Machine Press* and in the U.S.A. at Caleb Puckett's *Futures Trading*. The story cycle *Poison and Antidote* appeared online in Prema Bangera's *Wilderness House* and in Red Ochre Press's *Black & White*, edited by James Akers. "Testament of Faith" was featured in the inaugural number of George Filipovic's online *One Throne Magazine*. "House Hunting" found a space in *Streetlight Magazine* under the editorship of Suzanne Freeman. "With Paul at the Beach" appeared in *Forge*, edited by Melissa Venables, and, before I could withdraw it from consideration, also in James Esch's *Turk's Head Review*. (Sorry about that, Melissa and James.) Lastly, "Lilith" returned to the Bay Area in *The Bicycle Review* under the editorship of J. de Salvo. I thank all of these editors and journals from the bottom of my heart for their time, consideration, and support. The story cycle *Poison and Antidote* originally appeared, many, many moons ago, in a considerably rougher form, in Jeff Gburek's *Aql* magazine. A most heartfelt thank you goes out from me to Jeff for his support, perspicacious criticism, and friendship these many years. Debra A. Zeller, M. E. Evans, Marc Gilson, Kathleen Nichols, and, particularly, Carla Christenson and my fabulous editor, Brian Parks, all read drafts of these tales and helped to make them so much better than they might have been otherwise—my deepest gratitude to each and every one of you. A second nod is also due my partner and cover designer, Debra A. Zeller: the next one, my love, will be for you.

This book is for both my parents and the kids,
especially my own, Edoardo James Foust.

POISON AND ANTIDOTE

"Low types they must have been,
their pockets full of poison and antidote."

—SAMUEL BECKETT
The Unnamable

"...One might have thought her dead already
but for the terrifying, ever-faster movement
of her ribs, which were shaken by furious gasps,
as though her soul were straining violently
to break its fetters."

—GUSTAVE FLAUBERT
Madame Bovary

1: GROWING UP

No, I won't open my eyes. I'll roll over, settle back in, and get comfortable again. I won't be delivered; I'll try to go back to sleep. But I probably won't be able to, now that I'm this awake.

Let the eyelids lay; keep 'em forced shut—seeing the orange, the red of the sunlight through the curtains—there isn't any reason to be right now, despite daylight. There's no point in turning over, either, only to have to settle back in again. Still, this now: thoughts I can't help but see, unavoidably—

Always, from this morning on, whenever I walk out into the streets, I'll grab any interesting face I find by the nose and pull the features forward with my left hand. Then, when the skin begins to separate from the sinews and the web of muscles behind it, with my right hand I'll raise my hatchet high and slice downward from the forehead, pulling the face away from the skull by its nose, taking the startled expression up into the air and stuffing it into my burlap sack.

In the evenings, when I return home, I'll paste the faces—trimmed around the edges so that they resemble masks—in rows upon the white walls of my kitchen.

My mother, being afraid of strangers, doesn't approve of my collection. She throws her head back, her nose into the air, and says, "Must you bring those things into the apartment?"

My collection of eyeless expressions remains incomplete, though, without mother, so I've reserved a space above the stove for her disapproving face. Someday she too will stare out over the pots and pans, her dried skin coated in the ever-falling dust that's glued to her features by the greasy fumes from the frying pan below, labeling my life a failure with her unshutting eyes.

These days she asks me over and over, "When will you ever grow up?" And is afraid—being always afraid of death—that someday I really will.

HOUSE HUNTING

The first thing you need to do is case the neighborhood, check out the streets in the area, walk around between the buildings—imagine yourself passing by these same sights every day. You have to be lucky too. You have to imagine yourself coming home to the apartment, wanting to go back, night after night, yours for better or worse. You don't want to be driven out sooner than you feel like going. You have to be prepared for what it might do to you, how it might make you feel. You have to love it a little before so you don't hate it later.

The place I was looking at that day was down South of Market, in the old industrial part of town—which is a kind of schizophrenic neighborhood, too, having little bits of the other parts of the city in it as well. I was walking around and under the freeway that skims above the cross streets—it's too low down here to have any buildings beneath it—and then arches up to become the Bay Bridge further along, cutting through the even-numbered piers on this side of the Ferry Building. I was figuring out the topography of the neighborhood, its low warehouses and typical San Francisco-style three-floor Victorians, the old established wholesale businesses leaning up close to the sidewalks, jumped-up new factory outlets behind renovated Art Deco façades and minimalist parking lots, a few grimy liquor store/corner markets, and the occasional deli for the local employees to lunch at.

Of course the bars: the anonymous final resting places of derelict alcoholics on Fifth Street between the dirty magazine newsstands, the pawn shops, the window-barred liquor stores, and the boarded-up storefronts of failed businesses; the scattered gay and lesbian nightclubs fanning out toward the Mission District, hip and cliquey. There's the disco-pounding Stud, nude-dancing Clementina's, and the leather bikers' enormous S.F. Eagle. The Eagle had a sign out that day, "Slave auction tonight!"

These underground spots would pave the way for what was to become the club-going center of San Francisco in the late '80s, but on the day that I'm talking about there was only the silly discothèque with the swimming pool, the Oasis, and a brand-new, hip, post-punk art-school restaurant called the Billboard Café. Above all these nondescript warehouses poked the one edifice in the whole neighborhood that could challenge the freeway for height, the pink stucco church at Tenth and Howard. The shrine next to it—behind the low stone fence and the well-groomed lawn, with the Madonna and child nestled in a Plaster of Paris cave, also pink—always reminded me of the eighteenth hole in a miniature golf course.

I decided, that day, that I liked the South of Market and that I *did* want to live there. It's one of the real parts of the city, a whole landscape that just happened over time and completely by accident. Other parts of San Francisco have been made, claimed, and then cultivated by one demographic or another, like the Haight-Ashbury by the hippies or the Castro by the gay community, but nobody had ever cared enough about the South of Market or the Mission or even Downtown really to make them over completely.

I walked along, looking closely at everything and seriously considering the neighborhood for the first time, trying to imagine myself living there through the summer, the fall, and the rainy winter—I was wondering how it would change with San Francisco's subtle seasons. In my baggy pants and thrift-store overcoat, walking in the fog past the old buildings, wet and gray, I remember the day like a scene from a '40s film noir. I probably looked a little like Sterling Hayden, all tall and loose as I am, or maybe, being alone and eyeing everything so suspiciously, I came off more determined, like a desperate Richard Widmark character. Inside myself, though, I was feeling cool and glib, like my hero, Robert Mitchum.

The wind was cold, and it made me walk faster after a while, although I knew that it would eventually blow the fog away—thinking about that was already cheering me up. I pushed my hands against the seams of my overcoat's pockets and felt myself grinning excitedly as I found the street where the apartment needing a new roommate lay in wait for me and I went around the corner. It was a beautiful and tragic back alley, quaint and decaying; it dead-ended underneath the freeway in a parking lot cul-de-sac, a wash of trash blown into a sagging cyclone fence bordering the uneven blacktop.

Anticipation grew as I counted down the numbered cross-streets along Folsom Street to the tiny alleyway where I would be meeting my prospective housemates. You know how it is when you're house hunting—you guess it's that building up ahead, the one with the great big windows, or the one across the street with the enormous stoop, Corinthian columns, and ornate woodwork dappled by the only shade tree on the block. You're expectant or disappointed as the apartments vary from cramped modern cement jobs to well-painted Victorians with high ceilings and bay windows. I mean, style is important; it's the mood that the place puts you in that counts most the first time you see a place. I pegged the site of my appointment, disappointingly, almost as soon as I rounded the corner. I knew its type: a sprawling turn-of-the-century affair—probably built in a hurry as earthquake relief housing in '06—more long than tall, a shitload of tiny units crammed inside. The building started at the dead end of the alley but stretched about a third of the way along the block toward Folsom. Somebody had painted it yellow.

Once there had been four open-air stairwells, two doors to a floor, two floors to the building, old Western movie boarding-house style, but the stairs had been too secretive, dark, and inviting for this secluded alleyway, so the landlord had put protective cage-like metal gates over their entrances at street level. A panel of buzzers hung by each gate; one of them corresponded to the address I had in my hand.

I stopped and looked quickly around and decided that this wasn't such a bad block. I liked the randomness of everything in the SOMA, as it was only beginning to be called in those days, the neighborhood's openness. Garbage isn't as conspicuous in its wider, more commercial avenues as it is in the narrower, tree-lined streets in North Beach or up on Russian Hill. And the alleyways that crisscrossed the area were quiet and cool; they didn't scare me like the noisy Tenderloin sometimes did, with all of the frenetic resentment and opportunity-seeking stares of the malingering, self-proclaimed con-men, drunks, and whores. Anyway, the grime in the air is the same all over the city, even if the black dust maybe settles a little thicker on these derelict back alleys that probably never get cleaned. At least there's a place for the drunks to piss: in the parking lot down at the end of the street, instead of their having to do it in your doorway. It was ugly down at this alley's end—sterile, cemented, and blacktopped, looped around by that defeated fence and some tangled-up barbed wire, nothing growing in the shadow of the freeway. You almost couldn't hear the traffic up above, even though you were right underneath it.

SOMA was, at that time, according to the hippest intelligentsia, the up-and-coming part of town. There were already a few artists' lofts, renegade after-hours clubs and the Billboard Café, and more cool stuff would probably follow. Things were going to be happening here, and if I could get in on the scene right as it was about to explode... Also, it's the last part of the city to get the fog.

I didn't hear anything when I pushed the buzzer—once white, now smudged with greasy black newsprint fingerprints—so I knew right away that the apartment was up on the second floor. I felt bad about the interview being on a day like this; the lumpy summer clouds, remnants of the nighttime marine layer that caresses the city with the darkness, were still loping by just overhead, pressing down on the squat buildings of the area. I watched the gray globs moving inland, away from the city toward the bay, and knew that I liked places a lot less when I saw them on overcast days. But, then again, I'd seen some pretty ugly places look at least cheerful because of a sunny day, so I suppose it all evens out in some weird, unfair way. This place was starting to feel bad already, but I was determined to give it a fair shake.

There were so many things to be considered then, and it was hard to make a lot of firm decisions about the future. I was afraid of doing something wrong because it seemed suddenly to matter more if I did. It was like a test of myself somehow, of what I could do alone.

I heard a door open above, the sound of scampering feet coming down the stairs, and then a face blinked into view and looked out at me from the shadowy stairwell behind the bars. It was Christ, a typical hippie look: blue eyes against dark skin in a bony face with a beard of sorts. "Twenty-three A?" he asked, with a Latinate "Ah" sound for the letter A. I nodded, and he said, "Follow me," motioning with a single finger, turning his slightly stooped back on me to remount the stairs, his skinny arms dragging him along the handrails. I followed, his leather flip-flops slapping in my face as we climbed.

The roommate referral service had advertised my prospective housemates as Enrique and Miguel, and I was already having visions of sharing a South of Market loft with a young Picasso and Juan Gris, of pitchers of sangria and intense aesthetic conversations lasting 'til dawn, presided over by dark and passionate canvases leaning against the walls. Instead the film was in color now, unpredictable as a Godard or a Fellini, crazy and mannered, from the early '60s but definitely pre-Beatles—without irony.

The apartment was a cramped mess. Some loud and completely uninspired hillbilly rock-and-roll or Claptonesque dreck came from a department store stereo on the floor of what passed for a living room—really just a wider section of the hall. Other than the stereo, the room held only an imitation leather recliner and a knee-high stack of old *Playboy* and *Penthouse* magazines.

My guide showed me to the soon-to-be-empty bedroom, which was way too small for my stuff and had only a single dirty little window high up in one corner, letting onto an internal air shaft (or, as we usually call them on the West Coast, a light well). After glancing at the cell-like room, I followed Jesus back into the kitchen at the dead end of the hall and there he picked up where my buzzing of the doorbell had interrupted him, making soup using a Styrofoam Cup O' Noodles mix as a base.

I sat down at the table where he was working, chopping and mixing various ingredients. Behind my guide's silhouette, two enormous and frail-looking windows let in the flat gray light that came from the still solidly cloud-covered sky. The view was vast: a sharp, silvery, bran' spankin' new warehouse and a vacant lot filled with tall reeds and cattails. I found out later that this shadowy space between the buildings was the easiest and most frequented spot for shooting heroin South of Market, that it was San Francisco's own Needle Park.

"I am from Italy," Jesus told me. "I am the one moving out, moving up to Oregon." We had passed one of the roommates in the hallway, as he'd come out of the shower, and I'd introduced myself. This was the Enrique of the apartment's listing. While the towel-covered figure went off to his room to get dressed, the Italian told me that Enrique ran the household and shared the front room with his younger brother, Miguel.

Now we began chatting about working and living in the country versus the city, Jesus having much trouble finding the English for what eventually came out as, "I don't see how you can live all the time in the city. Is crazy, crazy." I asked him where he'd grown up and he'd told me in a "small village," as he chopped up much garlic and onions for his soup. "Real Italian soup," he grinned, enjoying grinning. "You like garlic?"

"Mmm, very much."

"It is, you know," he shook his knife at me, "the oldest antibiotic. Antibiotic—but natural. If you get a, a cut, on your arm," he held out his arm, nodding and gesturing toward it with the knife, "and you rub garlic or onion on it, it will stop the infection. I learn that in India."

"What were you doing in India? Working? Or just traveling?"

"Working? No. Is impossible to work there. Well, possible," (grin), "but… I do some business, mostly I was there for travel."

He chopped his garlic and onions leaning over, his spine curling under his tank top in all his deliberate concentration. I marveled at his Summer of Love outfit: the sandals and tank top, bell-bottomed pants that hung too low, a little wooden cross on a loose string of beads dangling in front of us, off of his neck. There was a patch of colored cloth holding the cross to its string of beads.

"Are you from the city?" he asked me, having apparently adopted the local habit of calling San Francisco simply "the city."

"No, not originally. I grew up out in the suburbs, but I've lived here for about two years now. Why are you leaving? You're going up to Oregon, you said?"

"Oh, well, I was before in Mexico, and before that in Guatemala."

"Did you work there?"

"Yes, a little, but the Mexicans work for very little, so I came here," he chuckled, "for the American green." He rubbed two fingers together with the grin still grinning and the blue eyes now widening out of the dark, bearded cheeks below the curly black halo of his hair. "Green American money." And we snickered together.

"I know what you mean." I still had punk-rock slogans on my T-shirts, but I'd been unfaithful lately I knew. Things were changing; I was getting older. It was gray, slow, and airy in that back room: walking into it had been like watching a long Sven Nykvist tracking shot from a Bergman or later Tarkovsky film. Now it had settled into a typically symmetrical Antonioni long shot depicting the alienated decadent face to face with the humble country peasant, the busy worker standing and working, the idle artiste sitting across the table watching him. If I'd thought about it, I guess I would have felt a little bit embarrassed. Still, we lived in the same shit neighborhoods in the same town and worked the same shit jobs to survive, so what was there to feel guilty about?

Enrique came in then, his hair still wet, perfumed, and all dressed up to go out. "So, did you show him the room and everything?"

"Uh-huh," the Italian and I nodded together.

"Yeah," I began, trying to be polite. "I think the room is too small for all of my stuff." Only the night before I had been up in Pacific Heights, San Francisco's swankiest neighborhood, charming two guys with the same politeness, and I would have that place (for the same rent as this one!) unless the third guy who lived there, who I hadn't yet met, decided for sure he'd rather have a woman move in. But Pacific Heights—although lovely with its wide residential streets, trees, Victorian mansions, and views out over Cow Hollow and the Marina—was a little like moving back to the suburbs.

Enrique smirked at me and said, "I thought so. Didn't you read, on the sheet, it said that the room was small?" He kept on smiling, speaking toward the wall, as if I'd already gone but, even absent, could still hear his insinuation that I probably thought I was too good for their apartment. I didn't remember their listing saying anything about the size of the room, but I'd looked at like a thousand listings that day.

"Yeah, I did," I stood up, "but I've lived in places where I could keep some of my stuff in the living room or something, and I thought it was worth a look." I was only just beginning to realize how easy it'd been to talk to and charm the guys in Pacific Heights the night before and how boring and stupid it would be living up there with them. But here I was kinda lost.

Enrique's smirk broadened into a grin when I put out my hand to shake. He ignored the gesture, turning away, but that was fine 'cause I really didn't want to shake his hand—only I didn't know what else to do. "I didn't want to run off without saying anything, so I waited 'til you got out of the shower to tell you in person." As we spoke, the Italian sang along with the record that was still blasting in the living room, adopting a kind of Southern accent in imitation of the rock band's undistinguished singer. I only became conscious then that we'd been shouting the whole time and ignoring the din.

Finally I got to the door, Enrique still smiling, insulting me without insulting me, not saying anything anymore, and the Italian winked at me as I fled. I threw a smile in his direction, went down the hall, out, and back up the alley to Folsom Street. It hadn't warmed up much yet, but you could feel the sun beginning to burn through the clouds. I could even see a little patch of sky out over the bay where the fog had already been blown away, so I walked off toward where the clouds were breaking apart, up Folsom in the direction of the bay and the South of Market piers. I didn't have any more appointments that day, and I wanted to think about all of the places that I'd looked at so far. There was one apartment in North Beach where I'd been interviewed that I wanted badly, and there was always the place in Pacific Heights, I guess. Odd that it was so affordable.

As I came over the crest of Rincon Hill, the fog was breaking up right over my head, moving fast in the breeze, and the sun came out and lit up the street around me at last. I stopped, took off my overcoat, and tilted my face up toward the underbelly of the Bay Bridge to feel the heat of the sunlight. From so close beneath it, the bridge loomed, huge and plastic looking, unreal, casting its long shadow the other way, toward the Financial District. I looked down the hill at the South of Market piers and saw that two of them, the ones just to the right of the bridge, had been leveled. I'd seen it on the news a few weeks before, but hadn't been in this part of town since then and had completely forgotten there had been a fire. Two long docks of black debris poked out into the greenish water, part of a steel infrastructure still leaning—black lines like a silhouette—on the cement foundations.

Next to the site of the disaster, just off of Third Street, a tacky-looking bar and grill called the Boondocks perched on the corner end of the burnt-out pier with what must be a great view of the blackened rubble out of its bayside windows. So I walked down the hill to the water's edge, went into the Boondocks, asked for a beer, and sat in a booth in the back by the windows to look out at the devastated piers and the almost fluorescent green water warming in the sun. The waves were only the tiniest little lines coming in absolutely evenly and then breaking apart against the pylons underneath the bar somewhere.

"Beautiful day, isn't it?" the waitress asked, coming close enough for me to see that she was older than I had thought—watching her come in earlier, talking and joking with the regulars up at the bar— but she did a good job of hiding it by smiling a lot and chatting happily all the time and using a lot of makeup.

"Yeah, it was cold when I was out there, and then it got sunny as soon as I came in here." We were both looking out the windows at what was left of the piers. "That's something."

"Sure is," she said. "Did you see that little place right on the edge of it?" About ten feet from the black pavement and charred piles of debris sat an old, drooping little diner called Red's Java House.

"Yeah, he must have been sweating. Well, I guess you people probably were too."

"Oh, I didn't work here then. But they said that it got hot." She reached out, pressing her palm flat against the glass of the window in front of me. "That if you touched the window, it could burn you."

5/1984
San Francisco

2: DAYS IN BLACK AND WHITE

There were probably days of color then, that autumn, sharper in the cold that blew itself in from the ocean. I noticed the change this time—the wind pushing brittle leaves and shreds of paper across dusty sidewalks. Things became new for me, for new reasons; I mean I changed.

I gave up waiting for buses and stopped picking up my mother's phone when it rang. I went out walking at night, looking into the well-lit windows of apartments and flats, always ending up out at the ocean. I caught my breath staining the air. There was a rhythm, walking, sometimes humming a tune I remembered, guys driving by with the radio cranked up. I should have tried to get to the desert. It wasn't all that far away and I've heard it's a good place to get lost.

It was twilight always, or it felt like it, in those streets—like in a de Chirico painting. I started seeing things through again, not only avoiding. I

15

turned my head to look directly at those things just on the edge of my vision, in the corner of my eye—but they weren't any different once I moved them into the center. It could be that boredom drives one to a kind of madness of minute observation.

I couldn't be alone all the time, but I tried. I wanted no urges. I crossed out smiles and was bored out of tears. The goal was to become as realistic as an animal.

I put on a show for the others, those who still managed to get through to me. But I didn't give anything away; I read a lot of books, stored up a million words and used them to build a few one-way bridges. I was reserved, in love.

Fashionably alienated, I might have grown into poetic dimensions—a man at last. Something made. The days themselves could have become different, summertime by now; I might have been persuaded into the sentimental life of those who stay so long they become legends in their neighborhoods.

JOHNNY'S PARTY

His nights were becoming harder and harder to fill. "It's all the goddamned thinking I do," Simon says to his empty apartment, "especially after dark. It slows everything down." He's sitting at the desk in the bay window of his Downtown studio, watching the blinking sign in the window of the State Garage across Leavenworth Street. Sam, his roommate, has gone away for the weekend, so there's no one to talk to. Simon has already eaten dinner and washed all the dishes and it's still too early to leave for Johnny's party.

He paces through the double doors that they'd dug out of the basement and re-hung between their two rooms to give the place the illusion of being big enough for two people. He goes from the main room of the glorified studio into the dining room, which acts as Sam's bedroom. He climbs out the window and onto the fire escape. Strangely, there's not much wind on this side of Leavenworth—even though the day's ending and the air's cooling in the San Francisco

17

summer evening's inevitable onslaught of fog. The city is halfway sunk in gray, now that the sun has set, and the streets are shadowless and flat below his second-floor perch, dotted with streetlights, neon, shop windows, and headlights. It's pretty quiet up here, except when the diesel buses strain up the hill every twenty minutes or so. Down at the corner the cars flow regularly along Sutter Street, taking workers away from the Financial District toward the Richmond and Sunset neighborhoods and their long rows of identical houses. Simon sits listening to the humming pulse of the car engines; the metallic throbbing that follows each cycle of the traffic lights.

He crawls back inside and puts on the Violent Femmes first record, loudly. It's a little early, but he starts getting ready to go to the party anyway. He sings along with the record, also loudly, cupping his palm around his ear to see if he's hitting the occasional note. He brushes his teeth, showers, dries his hair—bending over to get it to stand up—changes his clothes twice, and still it's only eight-fifteen.

Finally, reluctantly, he goes upstairs and rings Leila's doorbell.

"Hi." She's sort of smiling, not surprised to see him.

"Hey, Leila, what's up? You still want to go to that party I told you about the other day?"

"It's tonight?" She cocks her head, pondering. Simon watches the light coming down the hall behind her shining through the red cellophane job on her hair.

"Yeah, tonight."

Razor cut short on the sides like a boy's, Leila's hair stands up high, permed on top, one big curly lock in the front—which she now tries to brush aside—falling across her forehead. "What time?"

"It's supposed to start after nine, but I'm kinda bored so I thought I'd head over there now. You know, it's my friend Johnny's party, so I'm sure we could get a drink or something and hang out with him. Or, if you want to, we could stop and have a drink at Squids or someplace on the way."

The air coming out of Leila's hallway smells of cigarette smoke and brand-new carpeting. Simon has never been past the doorway, but her apartment must have the same floor plan as his and Sam's place directly below. Often he lies in bed listening to Leila walking around upstairs in heels, hears her muffled voice talking on the telephone.

She lifts and turns the hand holding the cigarette to check the time. Although she appears unaware of it, a lengthy tail of ash dangling from the cigarette does not fall on the new carpet. She's wearing a cute Esprit pseudo-'40s patterned Rosie-the-Riveter-style blouse. Behind her, a television mumbles steadily down the hall from the main room, spraying colored light and shadows across the walls. "I don't know," she says, "I'm pretty tired. I think I'll take a nap now, or a bath, and go over to the Club Anon or the Sub Club later. Sorry, but, you know, after working all day..."

"No problem. I'll probably end up at the Sub Club later too. Maybe I'll see you there."

"Yeah," she smiles, brightening her face in Simon's direction, happy to be off the hook, tilting her head in the other direction now.

"So long."

"Have fun."

Simon trots back downstairs to his own apartment, only there isn't anything to do there, so he locks up and goes off to Johnny's party a little bit early.

Instead of jump-starting the oversized moped, Simon gets on and lets it roll down the hill toward the Polk Street gulch. He pulls the clutch as he passes through the intersection and the motor kicks in. It'd been a warm day and the bike runs, for once, without stalling. He circles around Polk to Grove, which is wide and one-way and where there's less traffic. At the top of Cathedral Hill the wind blowing in off of the ocean hits him head on, slowing the bike to what feels like a standstill, forcing water out of his eyes and then pushing the tears back across his face. On the downside of the hill there are more Victorians, more of old San Francisco, much more dilapidation, garbage, and people out on the streets. He has to detour around Alamo Square to get to Johnny's place further out in the Western Addition, just off of Divisadero. A black neighborhood since the end of World War II, white punks, students, and artists had begun moving into the area, trepidatiously, for the cheaper rents.

Simon finds Johnny's block pretty easily, but he can't remember the exact number, figures he'll see the lights or hear the music from the street. He locks the moped to a street-cleaning sign in front of a Laundromat on the corner. Some teenage hardcores are making themselves noticed, coming noisily up the street behind him. One's carrying a sealed bottle in a paper bag. Their voices and gestures are purposely exaggerated and always on, aimed at annoying the uninitiated. Simon follows them up to Johnny's building and then inside. They must be friends of Severus's, he imagines. Fucking bullies. Man, when I was a punk we were trying to change the world. Severus is one of Johnny's roommates; Simon hasn't met him yet, but he's heard stories.

Going up to the third-floor flat he has to step over a couple of people sitting in the long stairway talking, glances into the living room and dining room (which have been connected by opening the sliding doors between them), and finally finds Johnny and his equally slim and lanky Scottish girlfriend, Mary, in the kitchen. There are three other couples standing around in a circle, looking a little uncomfortable, smiling a lot. Simon realizes that these must be guys from Travis Air Force Base, where Johnny works, and their dates. Johnny's invited them, like some of the Haight Street hardcores, "to make the party really diverse."

Johnny Chan, born in Macao and raised in the public housing projects that tower over Stockton Street near the Broadway tunnel, until pretty recently a high-school punk, is now an electrician in the Air Force during the week and a well-known San Francisco scenester on the weekends. He's startlingly tall and slender, a straight-up black flat top exaggerating his height. He's wearing dark prescription glasses perched on the chiseled cheekbones surrounding the charming grin that has won him many, many hearts.

"Hey, Simon, did you come in just now?" Johnny's long brown hands cover Simon's, his plastic bracelets jangling, as he leans over him. "Where's your date?"

"Yeah," Mary adds from behind the kitchen counter, in her still lusciously strong Scottish accent, sitting on a high stool next to a friend. "Where's the lass who lives upstairs you've been telling us so much about?"

"Oh, you know."

"Uh-huh," Johnny changes the subject by beginning to introduce Simon around. "So, let me see, this is Mike," he says, "and..."

"Elizabeth," the woman standing next to Mike says.

"Elizabeth," Johnny repeats, "Mark..." and so on around the circle of the out-of-place Air Force guys and their dates.

During all of the introducing, Simon takes notice of the hiply dressed and maybe slightly older woman sitting at the counter next to Mary. She's wearing a puffy blue early-'60s taffeta party dress with a low neckline, and is sporting a cute, curly hennaed bob, very 1920s. Getting closer to the woman, however, Simon notices that she's not any older than the other partygoers, it's just that she's been crying; her eyes are swollen and not focusing on anything in particular, circled red in the middle of her white, powdered face. Empty and half-empty beer and alcohol bottles rise up on the kitchen counter in front of her and Mary like a miniature city skyline. Simon goes over, surveying the bottles, figuring out where to begin.

"Gin, I think."

"What cheek not to bring the girl we've all been dying to meet," Mary says to him as he takes up the bottle.

"Well, she said she was too tired to come out so early after working all day." Looking closer at Mary's friend, as he pours, Simon decides she's either very drunk or stoned or something, but beautiful all the same.

"This is Johnny's friend," Mary says to introduce them, looking worriedly at her friend teetering on the counter stool.

"Hi," the woman says, her eyes not quite connecting with Simon's.

"This is my friend Dolores."

Johnny appears behind Simon, laying one of his long hands on Simon's thin-lapelled early '60s thrift-store blazer's shoulder, saying, "So, what you been up to lately? Haven't seen you for a while."

"Oh, hanging out."

"Yeah? Hey, let's see if we can get some of these people to move into the living room."

"Sure." Simon drops a couple of half-melted ice cubes into his gin and follows Johnny down the hall.

"Like the music? I made four mix tapes—it took me hours. I tried to pick only songs that were danceable but ones that you'd never think of as dance songs."

"Well, I like what I've heard so far."

Johnny lights a cigarette and says, "I wish people would dance. I guess nobody's really here yet."

"Yeah, where's the rest of the gang?"

"Don't know"—for a second he's annoyed—"being fashionably late I suppose."

Simon leans against the wall next to the gas-converted fireplace and sets his drink on the mantelpiece. Johnny's brought a bottle along, which he now puts on the mantle next to their drinks so he can dance. Looking through the sliding doors into the darker dining room, Simon sees the teenage hardcores lying around sharing a joint. They're spread out across the floor and furniture, forcing a kind of belligerent casualness, like they aren't used to their newly grown limbs yet. A couple of them are lying on top of each other on the sofa.

"Those are my roommates Severus and Pantha."

Johnny and Simon each take a slug from their drinks and Johnny asks, "So what's up between you and this lady?"

"Nothing's gonna happen. I mean, she seems to like me okay, as a friend or whatever, but I don't think I'm the type of guy she wants to go out with, or is used to going out with. You know, I don't have a lot of money or a car or anything, and I think those might be prerequisites for a girl like her. For Christ's sake, she works in the

Financial District." While explaining his situation, Simon watches Pantha and Severus rolling around on the sofa, their hands groping blindly over each other, their half-open mouths meeting up once in a while.

Seeing Simon observe his roommates, Johnny says, "Pantha's been on painkillers all week. She fell down the stairs and broke one of her teeth."

Pantha's eyes are closed and she's breathing noisily. Her furry mohair sweater is pulled up over her extended stomach, which looks more swollen than flabby. She's wearing a black mini-skirt and torn fishnet stockings, her body limp and sloppy inside them, unconcerned, heavy.

"Severus has been driving us nuts all week trying to take care of her. He's fucking paranoid. But I guess she *is* in real pain."

Severus turns over on his back then and laughs at the ceiling: Pantha's fallen asleep. He reaches over and picks up a bottle of tequila that he'd left sitting on the floor next to the sofa and takes a swig. Simon watches Severus's bare arm slide out of the sleeve of his tiger-striped horsehair vest, reach, recoil, and then stretch out again as he lifts the bottle, gulps from it, and rights it in its spot on the hardwood floor. There are lots of punctures and bruises on Severus's skinny forearm.

"So, how do you like the threads?" Johnny stands back to model his outfit. He's wearing a white dinner jacket, a paisley bow tie, a neatly pointing handkerchief peeking from the jacket's pocket, and plastic-looking patent leather shoes.

"Darling!" Simon teases. "No, really, you look great."

"Thanks." A new song, something that Simon's never heard before, starts on the tape; Johnny dances off across the room, motioning for Simon to join him. Simon takes a quick drink from his glass and follows, dancing toward the big bay window in the living room overlooking the street.

"Great tape."

"What?"

"This is a great tape. Where's the stereo?"

"In the other room. We ran the speaker wires out the bedroom window and into this one so no one could get to the stereo. We didn't want anyone fucking with the music while the party was going on."

Simon looks at the speakers and follows the wires out the open right-hand panel of the bay window. Looking through the glass and across the street, he suddenly notices all of the lights in the building over there.

"What's that?"

"Old folks' home."

"No shit?"

The building across the way is one of those modernistic cement block buildings so rare in San Francisco's Victorian neighborhoods. Each room presents a single, identical square window to the street; most of them are lit and some of the inmates are propped up in chairs to watch the goings-on up here and down on the sidewalk below.

"Look at 'em all."

"Yeah. Pretty funny, huh?"

A Joy Division song starts in with a crack of the snare drum and Simon says, "Hey, all right," moves away from the window and starts dancing again.

A few of the Air Force people have wandered into the living room now. They're curious but obviously wary of the street punks; they probably also think that it's kind of strange that their friend Johnny is dancing with Simon. They stand around in a little group looking at each other, nervously sipping at their beer bottles and shrugging.

"Hey!" Marguerite comes loudly into the party and gives Simon a quick but comfortable kiss. A stocky fellow all in black has followed her timidly into the room. Marguerite's a musician and an old friend of Simon's who grew up in L.A.: bleached blonde bob parted on the side hanging down over one eye, mascara, lipstick, a tight-fitting sleeveless '60s dress, breasts slightly, suspiciously too large for her skinny torso.

"Margarita," Simon says, Italianizing her name for the joke, "the princess of the pizza! What's up?"

"Simon, this is my friend Lex."

"Lex?"

"Uh-huh, Lex," he says, shaking Simon's hand.

"Pleased to meet ya."

Lex has a roundish shape, short red hair, a mustache, and a well-trimmed goatee hanging from his bottom lip. Soft spoken, he's always grinning. He's also wearing the uniform of the S.F. State film student: black blazer, black T-shirt, black pants—everything but the Eraserhead lapel pin.

One day out at State, a year or two before, Marguerite had winked at Simon and given him a flyer advertising a gig that her band was playing at a club over in Oakland. He'd gone to the show, they'd spoken there, and become lovers, briefly, before she'd blown him off for one of her new San Francisco roommates, Mick. Now she drops her purse in a corner of the room and joins Johnny and Simon's dancing, giggling in this slightly unladylike guttural way, happy to be a part of the group. Lex steps back to watch. "I'll get us some drinks," he says, disappearing down the hall toward the kitchen.

"So, what have you been up to, Simon, since the end of the semester?" Marguerite wants to know, dancing up close to Simon.

"Nothing much."

"Working this summer?"

"Yeah, in a movie theater over on Union Street."

"Work much?"

"Not too much, no."

Mary comes into the living room hurriedly and pulls Johnny away from the group of dancers, leading him out into the hall. Simon notices that, before leaving, she takes a rushed, worried look around the room.

"I wonder what's going on," Marguerite says.

"Who knows?"

Then they hear loud voices coming from the far end of the hall, near the back bedrooms, angry-sounding voices. Lex shows up at the same time with two drinks. "What's happening out there?" Marguerite asks him.

"Oh, it's all your fault, you party crasher," Lex says, handing her a plastic cup full of vodka. "Really, I don't know; some commotion over the bathroom I guess."

Simon downs a sip of gin and slips out into the hallway. He finds Johnny and Severus standing up against one another outside the closed bathroom door. Pantha is sitting against the wall in the narrow hallway, her knees pulled up to her chest, clutching her swollen cheek overdramatically. Severus's eyebrows and jaw are twisting strangely as he shouts and points his finger into Johnny's lapel, which is about level with Severus's chin. The door to the bedroom behind them is open and a bright light in there is making it hard for Simon to make out Johnny's forced calm features. It's also backlighting his flat top, which gives Simon the sudden impression of a mesa with the sun setting behind it towering over Severus's pimply pink and screaming face. For once Johnny's not smiling, which makes him seem particularly intense.

"This is important, man—Pantha's fucking in pain."

"Well, Mary's friend is having a hard time too." Johnny's voice is controlled, deeper than normal as he tries to speak calmingly to Severus.

"Fuck that, man, fuck it! She needs to get in there." Severus lunges suddenly for the door. Johnny grabs him and holds him back.

Simon, who had stopped a little ways down the hall, steps up now, but there doesn't seem to be any way for him to get into the scuffle. Mary comes out of the bathroom then, leading Dolores, who's obviously been crying, by the hand. Dolores's party dress has gotten all wrinkled and disheveled too; it's a little wide in the shoulders and one of the straps has fallen down across her bare upper arm.

"It's all—hey!" Mary slugs Severus on the arm, up by his shoulders. "It's all fucking yours!" She pushes him and Johnny out of the way and drags Dolores off down the hall. "Take it and fuck off, ya twat!"

"Yeah," Dolores sneers, pulling Mary back toward Severus. "Take your Goddamned bathroom!" Then she grimaces, her eyes going off somewhere but trying to focus—on what it's hard to say—streaks of tears still glistening on her face but no longer crying, "Use it to your heart's content."

Severus spits down the hall after them. Then, slipping out of Johnny's grip, he pulls Pantha up off of the floor and drags her into the bathroom. "That bitch," Pantha mumbles as Severus slams the door behind them.

Mary takes Dolores past Simon and into the living room to keep her away from the booze in the kitchen.

"What the hell was that all about?" Simon asks Johnny now that they're alone in the hall.

"Oh, Christ, they're so fucked up they can't think straight. Pantha needed to get into the bathroom to get her painkillers and Mary and Dolores were in there, that's all. They were going to be gone, man. I thought it would be okay. At the last minute they decided to stay because Pantha didn't want to miss the party. I can't believe it."

"Wow. What are you going to do?"

"Nothing at this point, I guess."

"And this friend of Mary's, she's beautiful. What's up with her? What is she, drunk?"

"Yeah, her best friend just died. I think she's been drunk since some time yesterday, or the day before, when she found out about it."

Back in the living room, Simon pours another helping of gin into his plastic cup.

"Hey, this party is pretty exciting," Marguerite says. Then, in Simon's ear, she whispers, "Quite exciting," giggles again from the back of her throat, leaning away from him, grinning, one wide blue eye not hidden by her hair.

"Have you been drinking, Princess?"

"Of course."

"So—other than school—what have you been doing? I haven't seen you in forever."

"You know, nothing—playing with the band."

"Who's this Lex guy? He looks like Victor Buono."

Marguerite laughs sarcastically. "He's okay. He's a friend of one of my roommates. He's into film or something."

"Where'd he go?"

"Probably into the dining room to gather material."

"I wish you people would dance," Johnny says, coming back into the living room.

"Simon," Mary pulls him away from the group, "would you look after Dolores for me for a minute? Don't let Pantha or Severus bother her, okay?"

"Sure." He finds Dolores propped up against a wall of the living room on a cushion, holding a plastic cup in the air at the end of her outstretched arm balanced, at the elbow, on her bent knees. "Hi," Simon says, sitting down next to her.

"Oh, hi, you're..."

"Simon. Johnny's friend."

"Hello, Simon." She puts out her damp left hand and Simon shakes it gently. They smile at each other and Dolores looks around the room again, her face growing concerned, perplexed when she realizes she can't focus on anything very far away.

"Come on you people, dance!" Johnny says passing by, gesturing with a bottle of gin in his hand. "I sure wish somebody had brought some scotch." He winks at Simon and holds the bottle out, offering to pour some into his glass. Simon gets his plastic cup filled and asks Dolores, "Gin?"

"Sure." She holds out her cup, to which Johnny adds a tiny dribble.

"Do you want to dance? Johnny keeps making these lifting motions at me."

"Sure." Dolores pushes herself up against the wall and Simon follows her out into the middle of the hardwood floor. That slow song by the Style Council that had recently flooded the college radio airwaves, "The Long Hot Summer," is sliding, enticingly, out of the speakers. "So, what do you do?" Dolores asks Simon as they dance up close, without actually touching.

"I'm working at a movie theater for the summer. Normally I go to school, out at State." Looking behind Dolores, Simon notices that Severus's friends have left the dining room and that it's turned into a kind of civilized little sit-down cocktail party in there. The hardcores have mostly retreated into Severus and Pantha's semi-outdoor bedroom (one of those wood-slat laundry room/stairway-to-the-backyard constructions attached to the back of almost every flat in San Francisco), where the drugs have materialized and their friends have gathered.

"Hmmm," Dolores says, dancing clumsily, then slipping. Simon puts his hands out, steadying her at the waist. She doesn't seem to notice, just regains her balance and keeps on dancing as Paul Weller croons, "It don't matter what I do, it don't matter what I do..." Simon takes his hands away from her waist slowly, watching her, wishing he had the courage to leave them there.

Pantha comes into the living room, sneering as she surveys the party. Behind her, in the hallway, Simon hears more shouting. From the couch in the quieter dining room Marguerite and Lex look up at Simon. "What's going on now?" Marguerite fake-whispers, all excited as the Sex Pistols' "Bodies" blasts out from the stereo in the other room, in a segue that changes the mood entirely—a credit to Johnny's mix-tape-making prowess.

"Sounds like Johnny and Severus again," Simon says, totally drowned out by the music. "I'll be back," he shouts in Dolores's ear—she's dancing a little ways away from him now, ska style, her head down. He pushes past Pantha at the door; she's standing in his way, looking him up and down as he slides by. He hears her laugh behind him, like she's snarling, as he goes down the hall. Rushing, he starts to feel the effects of the alcohol as he moves, so he slows down and steps carefully along the passageway stretching out in front of him.

Before he gets to them he hears Johnny and Severus in the bathroom screaming at each other behind the closed door. Simon knocks loudly, pushing the door open. "You okay, Johnny?"

"Yeah, fine. I can deal with it."

"And fuck you too!" Severus shouts at Simon.

"Okay, just yell, I'll be outside." Simon closes the door and walks toward the kitchen. There's a gigantic bag of popcorn on the table and he eats a couple of handfuls as he browses through the thinning and mostly empty bottles. Suddenly the thought of more gin makes his stomach want to jump up out of his mouth and run away.

"Damn, no scotch. No scotch, no scotch, and no scotch. Nothing civilized left to drink." Over the bottles, through the back door, he sees Severus's friends crowded around the former laundry room in a haze of smoke. A couple of people he doesn't know are hanging out in the kitchen talking. They seem very far away. They'd glanced at Simon when he'd come into the room and he'd nodded to them and they'd only gone on talking, ignoring him since then. "Vodka? No. Damned dirty potato water. Looks like it's gonna have to be beer."

That's when he hears the fight break out.

Simon goes running, as best he can, back into the living room, and finds the two women scrambling about and clawing at each other on the carpetless floor, Dolores still in her high-heeled party shoes, Pantha barefoot. People are standing around watching them, stunned—or mostly amused.

Television's "Marquee Moon" is playing on the stereo.

Simon observes for a second from the doorway and then pushes through the people, up to the fighters, and into their grappling. He shoves Pantha away from Dolores, screaming, "Fucking leave her alone!" He then drags Dolores a little ways away on the floor before Mary lifts her out of his hands, raising her up and putting her back down onto the cushion on the floor where she'd been sitting earlier. Dolores is twisting herself around to examine her dress, which has ripped up the back, along the zipper. The shoulder strap is down again, too, and Simon is standing there looking at the white skin of her neck flowing down her arms and chest, dotted with dark, foreign-looking freckles. In that instant the phrase "milk and honey" inexplicably enters his mind.

"You okay?" Mary asks, brushing her hand through Dolores's hair, holding her left, still covered, shoulder in her palm and shaking it gently.

"That bitch," Dolores says, reaching around to feel the back of her dress. "You bitch!" She pulls up the fallen shoulder strap, her eyes narrowing and glaring at Pantha—or at least in Pantha's direction. The strap falls again and Dolores looks at it in confusion, raises it again, mumbling, "All I was doing was crying in the fucking bathroom."

Everyone turns toward the door when Severus screams, from out in the hall, "What'd she fucking do?!" The living room is crowded now with curious people who are fast becoming scared people as Severus storms into the room and bears down on Dolores and Mary. Johnny's right behind him, trying to hold him back by the shoulders. He's been behind Severus all the way down the hall, keeping his hands on him and trying to talk some sense right into his ear.

Mary, screaming back at her housemate, pushes him away and tries to get in-between he and Dolores. When Severus tosses her aside, Johnny jerks him around, throwing him off balance. Severus tries to punch Johnny in the stomach as he falls, but Johnny's too big: He enfolds Severus in his gangly arms, pulling him down, and they tumble together across the floor to a corner of the bay window. Simon follows them but can't seem to catch up with or stop the rolling of the locked wrestlers, or do anything at all. When they come up against the low wall underneath the window, Johnny pins Severus, covering him almost completely with his own body. It's as if Severus is trapped inside of him, struggling upward to get out. This silly deadlock holds up for a few minutes, Johnny talking all the time in a low hum, the words impossible to make out because of the music pouring from one of the speakers turned on its side near Severus's feet—he gives it another kick and it slides up against the wall.

"I'm gonna let you up, okay? Are you gonna be okay? Are you gonna be cool?"

"___"

"What?"

"___"

"Okay, I'm letting you up." Johnny relaxes and Severus comes bursting up from underneath him, trying to get that punch in at last.

Johnny blocks his swing and shoves him back down, accidentally banging Severus's head against a panel of glass on one side of the bay window. The pane shatters outward and falls with a far-away tinkling onto the sidewalk below.

"Come on!" Johnny yells, covering him up again, "get it together, man, get it together!"

The deadlock holds for a long time this time, Johnny talking on and on as Severus wears himself out pushing and struggling against him and finally gives up. The people standing around slowly realize that the main confrontation is over and that things will only fizzle out from this point. They go back to talking or wander off to the kitchen to get something to drink.

"Marquee Moon" is still playing on the stereo.

Mary leaves the room and comes back wearing a big wool overcoat and carrying an overnight bag. "Come on," she says to Dolores, "where's your coat? Did you bring anything else?" She turns to Simon: "Tell Johnny we'll be at Stella's place for tonight." And, more excitedly, her Scottish brogue bursting forth emphatically, "Aye, and tell him we're moving out of here right away. I just can't have these daft things going on in me own house, where I have to live. I really can't stand for it anymore."

"Sure, I'll tell him," Simon says, walking them to the door. "I'll keep an eye on Johnny too."

As Mary and Dolores go down the stairs, they pass a group of Johnny's old high-school friends coming up, just now arriving. Adrian, who plays guitar in Johnny's band, leads the way, Eric and Rachel following.

"Adrian, hey."

"Hello, Simon—Simple Simon! What's up?"

"Where's Devin? Not with you?"

"Devin had to stay home with his wife tonight." Devin sings in Adrian and Johnny's band, the Troubled Wrecks. "And Lee, you know, our new drummer, he was supposed to come with his girlfriend, but I couldn't get ahold of him today to remind him. Did they by any chance get here by themselves?"

"Not that I know of. Hi, Rachel, Eric."

Eric swings into the room, pulling a long black cape off of his shoulders, flourishing it through the air and down onto the sofa. Underneath he's wearing a double-breasted suit jacket over a white shirt, a rhinestone broach holding the collar shut.

"Eric, how stunning," Marguerite gurgles excitedly, silently applauding his entrance.

"Thank you, Marguerite." Eric sits next to Simon, who he thinks is cute, and says, "We heard the glass shattering in the street and knew this must be the place." Simon and Marguerite relate the evening's events to the new arrivals while Johnny, the fight having finally worn itself out, puts on a hat and coat and goes off to Stella's to talk to Mary, promising to return as soon as he can. On his way out, he tells Eric that he's been saving the last little portion of a bottle of Stolichnaya for him and that he'll find it in the freezer hidden behind a bag of ice.

"I'll go with you to the kitchen," Simon says. "I've run dry again."

Eric pours the last precious drops of the vodka into a plastic cup over ice while Simon drunkenly grabs a beer out of a six-pack that some of Severus's friends are standing guard over. "Hey!" one of them yells after him as he runs down the hall and into Johnny and Mary's bedroom. Eric follows him, shutting the door behind them. Simon throws the bottle up so violently, laughing and gulping the beer, that the foam rises when he tips it back down and pours out onto the hardwood floor and toward Johnny and Mary's futon. Simon himself falls onto the futon then, letting his body roll over the blankets, laughing even harder.

Someone has brought the sack of popcorn in here and Eric kicks at it, sending little wads of fluff across the floor and into the puddle of beer. "What a mess," he says disgustedly, and then, "What kind of beer is that?"

"You mean on the floor?" Simon enjoys his own joke.

"No, in the bottle."

"All the same."

"Cooper's. Hey, that's going to be my alma mater," Eric beams. "Starting next year I'm going to Cooper Union in New York."

"Yeah, I heard that you were. For architecture, right?"

"Yes. And what are you gonna do with your life, Simon? I don't really know anything about you."

"Oh, I'm only working a summer job."

"Not going to school anymore?"

"I dropped out, I think. At least I'm not going back right away. My parents don't know yet—they're still paying my rent."

"What do you work at?"

"Nothing. Not now anyway. It doesn't matter."

"Is something wrong?"

"No, no." He takes a sip of the beer that's since settled back into its bottle. "This is pretty good stuff. I've never had it before."

"Hey," Eric says, finding something in the pocket of his blazer, "you want to do some speed?"

"No, not tonight. I feel like sleeping."

"Well, I've got to go get the others. I just now remembered I have the meth and they're probably all wondering where the hell I've gone with it."

Marguerite—Lex having left early, in the lull after the fight—Adrian, Simon, Rachel, Johnny—who's returned from Stella's—and Eric all crowd into Johnny's bedroom to do the meth behind closed doors. Someone burns a cigarette hole through the breast pocket of Simon's jacket while they're sitting there, taking turns bending over the lines with a rolled-up piece of paper.

"I guess we're moving out tomorrow," Johnny tells Adrian.

"Come stay at 86 with Devin and I. I'll be getting that new space down the hall in a couple of weeks, so there'll be plenty of room. And we could always use another hand for building once we get started on the new lofts." 86 Golden Gate, where Adrian and Devin live, in the heart of the Tenderloin, is up on the second floor of a commercial building rented by the square foot to a bunch of artists, musicians, and other freaks looking for open, flexible living spaces. The walls, lofts, electrical wiring, and even the plumbing of the place are all pretty much do-it-yourself.

"Devin and you aren't going to be living together anymore?"

"No, not now that we've both got a little money together. He needs more room to paint and I just want a space to myself."

"Are you gonna set up that recording studio that you're always talking about?" Marguerite asks.

Adrian nods, smiling, but he's actually thinking about his girlfriend who may move in with him and her plans for the new space.

Johnny leaves the bedroom for a couple of minutes, comes back and announces, "It's getting kinda hostile out there."

"Let's go for an alcohol run," Eric suggests. "That'll give 'em time to cool off and forget about us."

"My car," Adrian volunteers. "Come on, Simon."

Simon, Eric, and Adrian drive along Divisadero, across the panhandle of Golden Gate Park, to a late-night liquor store on Haight Street. From the backseat Simon sighs, "Look at all these stupid, freeloading street punks asking for change. Fucking dumb Marin County rich kids who think that running away from home and living off of somebody other than their parents is some kinda revolution. It's all about lifestyle these days, you know, image—they don't have a fucking idea in their heads. Man, when I first got into punk it meant something other than a clown suit, there was an idea behind it."

"At least they're not in fucking college," Adrian responds casually.

"Now, now—let's not be a sentimental drunk."

"Oh, fuck you, Eric," then, looking at Adrian in the driver's seat, Simon leans up and kisses Eric on the back of his clean-shaven neck.

"I'll get the booze and leave you two alone," Adrian says, hopping out and walking away from the car.

"I love putting him on," says Simon.

"You're such a tease."

"Uh-huh."

After parking the car, as they walk back up to Johnny's building through the foggy night air, the bottles jiggling in a bag in Adrian's hands, they each light cigarettes silently, contemplatively. They're soon shaken out of their stupor, however, when they find Severus braced across the doorway to the flat, his bony arm blocking their way, his head sunken, his tiny eyes peering up at them. "This is my house now," he rasps, "and you're not coming in."

Adrian, who was once a pretty good friend of Severus's, tries to talk him out of it, but they still don't get inside. They're finally reduced to screaming "Johnny!" up at his bedroom window. When he finally pokes his head out, Adrian tells him to come down, with everyone, and they'll all go somewhere else. They load Simon's moped into the trunk of Adrian's car and head off to Eric's apartment in Diamond Heights. There, Adrian mixes a big pitcher of martinis in a canning jar while Eric shows off the design he's been working on for a beach house.

"See, the theory is that the whole thing moves from chaos to order. I want all of the angles in the front rooms to be odd, and none of the shapes to match in either size or exact shape. In the living room, here, there'll be pipes showing, air vents and heating ducts exposed, stuff like that."

"Yeah, but that's so conceptual, will somebody be able to live in it?"

"Let me finish, Adrian, okay? The effect I'm trying to get is that as you move through the rooms toward the back of the house the angles will slowly come together, the pipes and stuff will gradually thin out and disappear, subtly, from room to room. Then, in the back bedroom, everything comes together. The bedroom will be perfectly square on all sides, a cube, and in the very center of the back wall there's a square window that looks out onto the beach and the ocean will make a straight line across the exact center of the window."

"Doesn't that depend on how tall you are?"

"Well, yeah, but close enough. Come on, Simon."

"But—"

"Don't worry, Adrian, it *will* be functional as well. I do want people to be able to live in it."

"Have you told Devin about it yet?"

"No, I haven't seen him for a while."

"Yeah, he'd love it," Rachel agrees, dragging primly on a cigarette. "But I've got to go, Eric," she says, kissing him on the cheek. "My lover's home by now and waiting for me."

"Don't wear her out, dear," Eric advises, walking Rachel to the door. She's the youngest-looking and quietest of the group. Simon figures that she was part of their old high-school crowd but isn't quite sure.

The energy of the evening seems to run out with the emptying of the pitcher of martinis. Simon and Adrian start talking about their favorite bands, Eric and Johnny about clothes. Marguerite tells everybody about her plans for a new band—in which Adrian has agreed to moonlight on guitar.

"Why didn't you bring the boyfriend along tonight?" Simon asks her. To which she shrugs, saying, "Oh, he's away this weekend visiting his family." Behind her, Adrian makes the figure of a square in the air with his index fingers and Simon chuckles.

"Time for me to get going," Johnny says. "I can't believe my party turned out to be such a disaster."

"Not your fault," Eric says, putting a hand on Johnny's shoulder. "I think we had fun all the same."

"Yes, yes," Simon says, and "let's go then."

"Give me a ride to Stella's, Adrian?" Johnny asks, and Adrian nods.

"Have to get your scooter out of my trunk," Adrian tells Simon.

They all walk out to Adrian's car, feeling revived by the damp, nighttime air, their senses sharp now but their thoughts slow and mostly non sequitur.

Lagging behind with Marguerite, Simon asks her, "Hey, could I spend the night at your place?"

She looks at him strangely, and he adds, "You know, since Mick isn't around."

"Here you go," Adrian says, opening the trunk. Johnny and Simon hoist the bike up and out and set it on the sidewalk. Adrian pushes the trunk shut and turns back toward the driver's side, waving nonchalantly. "'Night, dude."

"'Night, Adrian."

"Yeah, later, Simon."

"'Bye, Johnny."

Adrian's too-big car rumbles *sotto voce* through the otherwise silent neighborhood. It's uncomfortably quiet after the old '70s clunker puffs out of sight. Simon and Marguerite are left standing in the street where Simon has pushed the moped to start it. Simon's a little shocked at himself for asking what he's asked, but he assuages his conscience by assuring himself, and her, that it had been an innocent request, that he's only lonely. "You know, I'm sorry. I just didn't want to spend the rest of the evening alone is all. I've been having trouble sleeping lately. But, it's okay—don't worry about me. I'll live."

"I don't know what you expect. I don't want to fool around on Mick, but I still care about you a lot, you know? I don't think you're being fair. How do I know what you want?"

"No, no, that's not what I wanted. All that happened before—I mean, that was over between us a while ago. Look, I'm sorry I even brought it up. Never mind me, I'm just fucked up. Where are you parked?"

"Down here."

"Well, hop on and I'll give you a lift."

Simon jumps the moped, Marguerite gets on, and he coasts the bike down the hill to her car. They part with a warm but businesslike kiss and she drives off in front of him. He takes a left after a couple of blocks and turns in another direction, cruising aimlessly through the nearly deserted streets, avoiding the hills—the moped, which is built too much like a motorcycle and is heavier than its own engine can support, can't drag itself up most of them.

Finding himself aimed across the outer avenues toward the Presidio, he decides to check out the beach. He comes around the back way, from California Street down Lake to Lincoln Avenue, past the rows of fancy houses with lawns and shrubs out front and into the military complex with its enlisted men's apartments, to the windy, Monterey cypress-lined road overlooking the ocean. The fog is butted up against the cliffs so he can't see the water from the road, but he hears it hissing against the rocks and sand below.

He pulls the bike off of Lincoln and coasts down the driveway into the Baker Beach parking lot. He comes right down to where the pavement meets the sand, kills the motor and raises the too-heavy moped (which everyone mistakes for a scooter because of its size) up onto its stand. He walks away from the pavement, across the beach toward this new roar out there in the darkness—no sound coming from the housing or the road behind him. He sits down on the sand in the wind and watches the arc of ocean that's come into view below the fog. The dark cliffs of Land's End jut out over the water to his left, above the beach, and the Golden Gate Bridge shines through the mist with its orange lights to his right.

After a while the sky starts turning purple. He wants to stay and watch the sunrise, but he's too tired. He gets back to his apartment just as it's getting light. The streetlights are still on, though, he notices as he draws the thrift-store curtains across the bay window in his bedroom. He writes his roommate Sam a note not to wake him in the morning, no matter what. He unplugs the phone, gets into bed, and wonders how long he'll be able to sleep.

1985-6
San Francisco

3: LOOKING AHEAD

I must have been dreaming, last night, maybe just now, I can't remember. Only the struggle: shuffling back into another mother's arms. Looking away, in another direction, and then closing my eyes completely to the world they've built up around me.

Thoughts now, maybe answers later — whatever you have to have. This is easy, for the moment, eyes closed, words begetting words.

We're part of generations. Cursed by its forcing a name on us. Think of seeing it, your birth; crying, rolling in your mother's flesh, her food for you, christened in her blood. I see myself encircled, and dreaming out of it too, pulling faces from the crowd for some meaning. I knew that later I would have to turn against the triangle and away from mama, but come back to the ruins of my family as well.

I remember; I was a difficult birth. I wrote a poem but nobody understood it. I'll tell you — I refused to breathe. They forced a tube and air into my clogged lungs and pumped me up like a balloon. Somebody told me I should forgive them, laughing. Not now, not yet, not in the frenzy of the present tense.

I was incubated, then, in a box: a box with glass walls.

LILITH

She called herself Lilith when she used to hang out at the Deaf Club. That's where you might have seen her, or at the Mabuhay, the Temple, or the Club Foot, pushing her way through the mobs of punks, taking everybody on, always talking to somebody, whether she knew them or not, ignoring or sneering at the paintings on the walls of the underground all-night clubs that kept springing up and vanishing overnight in those days. You'd always find her slamming or pogoing at the front, right up under the makeshift stage, complaining loudly about the bands that were too artsy for her taste in the middle of their quietest songs—those she didn't know from her Art Institute days, that is—and parting the crowds with her powerful five-foot-two-inch body, halo of curly black hair, and loud sarcastic voice.

My friends and I were too young to be hip enough for the A-Hole, though, the club that Lilith took us to the time that I first got to talk to her. It was, I remember, a Saturday night at the Mabuhay Gardens. I was with these guys from the 'burbs—we were still in high school, but only just—to see the Dead Kennedys when she asked me for a light. I didn't have one 'cause I didn't smoke then, but she kept on talking to me after she'd gotten a light from somebody else.

Between sets, while Lilith and I were trading favorite local bands, Dirk announced that there was going to be an after-hours party at the A-Hole later on that night. He was still doing his MC shtick then, where the audience yelled shit at him as he leaned out over us from that tiny stage, the roly-poly impresario with the slimy little Hitler mustache, throwing back the deadly quips while we all sweated in a leathery, hair-sprayed heap up under his nose, pressed against the stage, almost touching the low ceiling with our spiky hairdos. And you'd be thinking: Holy shit, man, in a minute we'll all be dancing like crazy. I can hardly breathe now and I bet we're all fucking killed when the music starts, trampled under each other's feet...

Then the Kennedys would come on, launch into "Let's Lynch the Landlord," and everybody'd be up and going and it wouldn't be like that at all, more like we'd been set free finally from standing around so long bored in our cages. Suddenly we'd be careening through space, getting plenty of air and rolling affectionately off of one another, like a waterfall of people, everybody so light— unless somebody accidentally steps on your foot with their boot or something—helping each other up when we fall, and I'd be thrashing away right in the middle of it, feeling loved and happy for the first time in my angst-ridden teenage life—especially now, after Dirk had mentioned the A-Hole, because Lilith has asked me if I was thinking about going over there later on.

Obviously I was thinking about it—totally into it in fact—and after a few songs I go find my friends who have the car we came in to tell 'em about it and they agree to go over there after they see Lilith. So I'm thinking that, yeah, I'm hot shit, that this is it, I'm in it now, the S.F. punk rock scene! But I'm worried, too, because Lilith doesn't know yet that I'm from fucking Walnut Creek, only a weekend punk really. But now that I think back on it, I'm sure she could tell by looking at me 'cause that was before I had cut my hair and I'd probably only blow-dried it up in a messy burr that night and I'm sure it wasn't fooling anyone. Of course there was less of a punk uniform back in those days too. I mean, when I think of 1977 today, it's the year that punk broke and the Pistols arrived but, at the time, I think that it was equally important to me that Peter Gabriel had just left Genesis.

When the show was over, we stumbled out onto Broadway and down the ramp of the parking lot next door to squeeze sweatily into Jim's two-door orange Capri—I think this was the night that somebody got a "Mabuhay Gardens: Just Another One Night Stand" bumper sticker and stuck it crookedly across the side of the car— and off we go down Battery through the Financial District and past Market Street toward China Basin, right at the base of Rincon Hill, and to the A-Hole. Lilith was in the front seat, sitting in my lap, talking a blue streak and telling Jim which streets to take right after we'd already shot past the turnoffs.

We did find it, after a while, and were still like the first people there—except for those too hip to be at the Mab seeing the Kennedys in the first place. Jim parked on the deserted street across from the brick warehouse with the plywood sign "A-Hole" hung above the door. Somebody said, "This must be the place," and we all went running up endless flights of stairs—too drunk now to have any accurate sense of time or space—and into the big, open half side of the warehouse or cannery or hay loft or whatever the building had been before the port of San Francisco moved over to Oakland and left it vacant. Well, what it was that night was fucking pretentious. There were a bunch of art school snobs looking suitably bored, leaning against the walls, holding beer bottles and cigarettes right at the tiny tips of their precious little fingers, pretending they were San Francisco's answer to Andy Warhol's Factory.

"How were the Kennedys?" somebody on the landing asked me as I went in and "Fucking great!" I said without reservation, earning myself a few snickers. I went ahead and played up the Sid Vicious thing then, curling my lip and plowing unheeding toward the bar like some kind of infernal machine shaking itself to pieces. I had Lilith by the arm and yelled, "What is this shit?" into her ear, referring to the weird artsy music they were playing.

That was about all the fun we had that night, my friends and I. One two-dollar Budweiser later we were bored out of our brains, falling asleep sitting up against the walls in a dark corner all by ourselves—only the embarrassment of the art punks snubbing us and the feeling of being totally out of place kept us there while I watched Lilith, done with me for the night, darting around the room like a fish in a tank, making friends with everybody she didn't already know.

The next time I saw Lilith was like a year or so later. I came across her sitting alone in the sun on the grass in Washington Square one afternoon. By then I was living in the city, going to school out at State, and had cut my hair. I was still on my parents' payroll though.

Lilith had dark purple streaks dyed into her even larger and more viciously teased-out hair and the sun was lighting them up vividly as she lay on the grass reading Georges Bataille's *The Story of the Eye* with her sunglasses on. She didn't remember who I was but took my word for it that we'd met before, made me sit down, and we talked like old friends until her bottle ran out.

She complained about her hair, how it was already the color that most people were dying theirs, like the Siouxsie Sioux clones—did I know Keira? No? Oh well, doesn't matter—and how she didn't feel punk enough sometimes because, you know, what can you do with curly hair? I thought she looked pretty good though. She was wearing a black crepe thrift-store mourning dress, a ton of plastic Mardi Gras beads around her neck, and was sitting on a trashed jeans jacket with some dinosaurs and something in Latin stenciled on the back. It goes without saying that she wore oversized combat boots on her tiny feet.

She'd also added a nose ring since the last time I'd seen her. She showed it to me close up and told me how she wanted to get more piercings—how she'd heard that sex was amazing after you'd had your labia done.

Then she wanted to know where we should go 'cause it was starting to get cold.

"I'm sticking around North Beach for a show at the Savoy Tivoli tonight," I told her. "You know, the café with the patio over on Grant."

"They're having shows there now?"

"Yeah, they've opened up this big room in the back. You're welcome to come with me if you want."

"Oh, I know—follow me," Lilith said and I bounded along behind her up the side of Telegraph Hill. She took me to the little record store on Grant Avenue and showed me the *Music From the Deaf Club* LP because she was in one of the photos of people hanging out at the club on the insert, wearing a leather jacket with a bunch of buttons on it and smiling cutely.

"Your hair was shorter then."

"Yeah, I was trying to get it to lie down with about a ton of mousse. It's so sad the Deaf Club's closed," she sighed, putting the record back in the rack. "It was my favorite place to hang out."

"Really, it's closed?"

"You don't know anything."

"Well, I always liked the Temple Beautiful, and it's closed now too." That's where I'd been to my very first punk show. My friends from out in the 'burbs and I had seen an ad in the pink section of the *Chronicle* that a band called the Dead Kennedys was playing at a place called the New Wave A Go-Go, and we thought that the name of the band was so funny we had to go see what they were like. We drove all the way into the city, through the Civic Center, and out Geary Street and were amazed to find that the club was a stately old synagogue! They'd cleared out the pews and pushed them up against the walls to make a dance floor and they had put blue light bulbs in the Star of David on the ceiling and the bands played on the altar, which was all graffitied and shit. We, of course, got there super early—we always did 'cause Walnut Creek closes up at six (if it were ever actually open) and punk shows didn't even start until ten or eleven. When we walked into the cavernous space under the balcony (where people scored drugs and made out) there was hardly anybody there. The Bags, a band from L.A., were playing belligerently to the enormous empty space before them.

I had never seen or heard anything like it. I walked right up to the altar and put my elbows on the stage and my adoring head on my hands and the Bags' singer, Alice, dropped to her fishnet-clad knees and leaned right into my face with her dark eye makeup and bright red lipstick to scream the next couple of songs at me—until I got too self-conscious and walked back to the bar where my friends were hanging out. They were standing around, shyly wondering if they'd be able to get a beer without IDs. By the time the Kennedys came on, at around one, the place was packed.

After the record shop, still killing time before the show at the Savoy, Lilith took me to the black-and-white-checkered punk and New Wave boutique on Columbus Avenue, below Washington Square, where I stood around bored and embarrassed while she held forth with the nerdy-looking '50s seersucker suit and slicked-back hair guy who worked there—she must have known him from somewhere. Lilith tried on like a hundred outfits, and then didn't buy anything. Then she led me back across Columbus Avenue to the Italian market just off of the square, where we bought some beers, a couple of rolls, and a slab of cheese. We went down to the waterfront, then, to eat and watch the sun go down, Lilith leading me past Aquatic Park and up some stairs on that hill overlooking Fort Mason, to this little meadow that had been a gun emplacement aimed out over the bay during one war or other.

She was talking about getting a band together. "I write all these great lyrics, and I'm sure I could sing if I found the right musicians. You don't play anything, do you?"

"No, I'm no musician—sorry to say."

"I wanna meet someone who can teach me the guitar so I won't be one of those bimbo girl singers, you know. I want to fucking play!

"So, who are we going to see tonight?" Lilith continued, changing the subject.

"The Sleepers."

"Oh, Ricky's band—that guy's so wasted."

I was impressed that she'd actually met him.

The Savoy was packed when we got in. They were between bands so the lights were up and Tuxedomoon's "No Tears" was playing loudly over the P.A. The space in there was weirdly shaped because the café stuck into what would have been the square back room that they had made into a club, forming an open L-shape with another L nestled into it, giving the room two separate wings. The stage cut across the crux of the outer L in the corner. When the Sleepers came on everybody moved to the right-hand wing because Ricky Williams, the singer, had long stringy hair that hung down over his face and you could only see his right eye peeking out between the curtains of hair on either side of where it parted.

The Sleepers put on a great fucking show, totally intense, meandering along in a kind of heroin-induced psychedelic drift behind Ricky's deep, sort of twisted David Bowie vocals. He had this amazing style that always sounded absolutely spontaneous, like he was making up the words as he went along, but when you compared the records with the live shows, every word came out in exactly the same pitch, rhythm, and intensity. I heard that he never wrote down a lyric either, that he was practically illiterate. And later, before his next group, Toiling Midgets, broke up, I saw him sing a whole set totally out of sync with the rest of the band. They would finish playing a song and he'd go right on singing without them. The band, unable to communicate with him, just shrugged and started up the next song while he was still singing. Then, after finishing the previous lyric, Ricky would start the next tune from the beginning even though the band was already halfway through the number. I guess he was hearing a different music somewhere inside his head.

That night at the Savoy, though, he was perfect, not necessarily stoned, but beautiful, and Lilith was entranced. "He's fucked-up, but he can really sing. He's some kind of a goddamned genius. What was that one song called again?"

"'When Can I Fly?'"

"Yeah, that's the one. Fantastic."

We walked out onto Grant Avenue after the show, where they were stacking the chairs onto the tables on the patio of the café. It was about two in the morning. San Francisco always falls asleep at that hour, when the bars shut down. The whole time I lived there I don't think I was ever awake past two-thirty or three in the morning. Lilith hustled me over to a liquor store to get a bottle before everything closed up and we went back to my flat to drink it.

In those days I was living with two housemates way up on Mt. Parnassus, just below the UC medical center on the edge of the eucalyptus grove underneath the Sutro Tower—which looms like an enormous steel insect, its feet dipped in fog, over that whole part of town. It was a long, two-transfer bus ride down to Market, out along Haight Street, then around the park to Cole Valley, and up the steep Parnassus hill. Lilith filled the journey with her voice, talking and telling stories and—totally inspired by the show we'd seen—planning for the band she was going to get together.

When we finally got to my flat she wanted to take a bath. "Come on, I feel all icky and sweaty from the club. It'll do you good. Where's the bathroom?"

I pointed it out and she dragged me down the hall, pulled me inside and shut the door behind us. I was kinda worried about my two housemates, both women, who'd rented me a room in their flat thinking I was a lot older than I actually was and who resented me a little, I thought, because I was such a kid to them. I hadn't lied or anything; they'd just assumed I was their age. One worked in an office and the other did social work. They subscribed to *The Village Voice* and it was from them that I first heard about feminism.

Lilith took a long drink from her bottle, cringed, and set it down carefully next to the tub, which was already filling with hot water. She made me unzip her dress in the back and shucked it off over her head. "Hey, come on," she said, yanking my T-shirt out from under my jeans. "Let's go—you're not going to take a bath with your clothes on."

I leaned over and she peeled the shirt off my back. Then she slid her panties down her legs and stepped into the tub while I sheepishly stepped out of my jeans.

I got into the tub behind her, trying to hide my hard-on. "Oh, look at that," she teased, grabbing hold of it. "We'll see what we can do about that a little later." She leaned back against me, making my blood rush, arched her neck and kissed me on the chin mostly— that was as far as she could stretch. Then she reached her arm up, took hold of my hair, pulled my head down and really kissed me, swiveling, pressing herself against me.

"Too bad you don't have any candles in here." She'd turned off the ugly fluorescent light and all we had was the glow of the city below reflecting off of the fog. Picking up the bottle from the floor where she'd set it down, Lilith nestled against me in the hot water, her hand still around the back of my neck, toying with the stubble. We lay there for a long time getting all shriveled up and listening to the foghorns low from across the bay.

When she was ready for bed, we giggled our way down the hall, wrapped in towels, carrying our clothes. She jumped into my bed and pulled me in on top of her as I tried to go past her to get to the stereo to put on a record. We started wrestling across my dirty sheets and she pinned me, straddling me with her legs, running her hands over me, pushing me down when I tried to raise up to kiss her, grinding her crotch into me. Then she shimmied up to my face, split her vagina with her fingers and pushed it up in front of my mouth. When she was ready, she turned herself around, sat down on my cock facing the other direction. She had barely begun to rock back and forth when I came. "Oh, bad boy," she said, slapping my thigh. But then she went on just the same until she came. I think I nearly fainted.

I was right, my roommates weren't happy about our noisy middle-of-the-night escapades, or the purple ring that Lilith's hair had left in the bathtub. They weren't happy in the morning either, when Lilith sat in our kitchen drinking coffee and smoking Camel straights until late afternoon, talking everybody's ears off. And they were even less happy when she came back in the following weeks, when she rang our doorbell at three in the morning after having closed some club or show, when she sat on our phone for half the day, calling people who hardly ever remembered who she was, or when she and some silent green-haired bicycle messenger friend hung out at our place all day while I was at school, smoking a blue haze all through the apartment.

By the end of the next month, with Lilith's help, I had found and rented a cheap studio at the back of a building on the Tenderloin side of Geary Street. Its only windows overlooked a parking lot with a view down Leavenworth's ever more depressing slope—from apartments, bodegas, and dry cleaners to bars, flophouses, and porno movie theaters. Some call those two or three transitional blocks between Geary and Eddy "The Tenderloin Heights," others "Lower Nob Hill." Whatever you want to call it, that's where we spent the summer, where I learned to smoke, to drink the rest of the bottle in the morning in my coffee, and where I learned to keep from coming until Lilith had gotten hers.

I got the night manager job at a used-book store in North Beach owned by a sleazy, red-nosed shyster who'd married an ambitious New Yorker, moved to Marin, and always wore a rotting Greek sailor's cap on his balding, devious little head. He spent most of his time adjusting our time cards in a downward direction and frantically searching for things for us to do during the night shift.

This usually entailed, despite the many complaints of our customers, moving the "Sociology" and "Technical" sections aimlessly from wall to wall.

That's when Lilith started hanging out in North Beach, in the flophouse hotels that were the real remnants of the Barbary Coast—not Melvin Belli's super-manicured hundred-and-fifty-year-old law offices. Where Nick, the drummer in Ricky Williams's new group, Toiling Midgets, took her when she ran into him in a café on Columbus Avenue. They were talking about her imagined musical future, so Nick decided to introduce her to Courtney, who was singing for a pretty popular S.F. band back then but was always looking for something better.

Courtney was physically the complete opposite of Lilith: tall and fleshy, wide-jawed, her dirty blonde hair clinging close to her head. She came off as a surly cross between Stevie Nicks and Joan Jett, her pale blue eyes turning off and on, the opposite of Lilith's dark eyes that couldn't stop staring right into you. They were kindred spirits all the same who recognized each other from the very first moment they met. They were always trying to out-talk, act more obnoxiously, and cause more trouble than the other—and get the better-looking boy to follow them home. The day Nick brought her 'round to Courtney's room, Lilith sat there pretending not to be amazed when Nick and Courtney tied up and shot some China White that Nick had scored from Cheryl, a dark-haired green-eyed half Sicilian who was dealing heavily in North Beach in those days, and who used to come into the bookstore to buy science fiction and decadent stuff like Poe and Baudelaire from me. I was also working with a couple of women who lived in those North Beach hotels and who were probably junkies too, but they didn't trust me enough to say anything about it.

Courtney lived up above Big Al's, Broadway's most famous strip joint, where the little red nipple-lights on Carol Doda's neon effigy blinked in her bay window, kitty-corner from the bookstore where I worked, which was next to Vesuvio's bar and across the street from my favorite hangout, Specs. So, you see, we were all centrally located to act out our little dramas in the close confines of a street and an intersection that became our whole world as Ronald Reagan toiled ceaselessly to take the rest of our country away from us un-American degenerates.

Lilith used to come with me to work in North Beach, spend the afternoon and evening hanging out with Courtney, or writing in her notebook in the cafés on Columbus Avenue, or in the park. She'd come into the bookstore around ten or eleven, grab a book and go upstairs to the office, where she usually fell asleep reading on the sofa. I'd come up after closing the store at midnight, wake her, and she'd pull me down and climb on top of me and we'd fuck 'til we were sore before going off to meet Courtney at the Mabuhay or the On Broadway, or at one of the newer clubs out in the Mission, or some all-night party down South of Market.

I have no idea exactly when Lilith started shooting drugs with Courtney and co. I mean, it's not as easy to notice as you'd think, and nobody was saying anything to me about it 'cause, obviously, I wasn't into their scene. I must have seemed pretty innocent to this crowd and I guess they never really took me too seriously. They probably thought I was kind of stupid, or too naïve to be worth corrupting, or something. The women I worked with were always sending their boyfriends to the store with stolen remaindered art books that they wanted me to buy at inflated prices. I usually paid them what they wanted because I couldn't have cared less, and, anyway, it was the boss's money and I hated the boss and all of his bullying. But I'm sure that they thought, in their junkie delusions, that they were putting something over on me.

Truth is, my mother had been a diet-pill popper when I was a kid and had pretty much beaten a healthy fear of drugs into me back then, so I wasn't much interested in joining their club. Still, I wasn't into morally condemning them either, so they put up with me for Lilith's sake, and 'cause I could drink, and 'cause I'd sometimes buy pitchers of beer at Specs for everybody. This seemed pretty natural since I was the one working and since I didn't have their extra expenditures.

But when that summer ended I had to quit the bookstore to go back to school and Lilith and I began to have less and less in common. She'd still come crash at my place after the bars and clubs and parties ("These our revels") were ended, but I'd already be in bed asleep a lot of the time and not very entertaining. I'd leave in the morning for school long before she ever woke up.

One day I phoned her at the bicycle messenger service where she had eventually gotten a job as a dispatcher. They told me that she was busy and that she'd call me back later—but she didn't. I called a couple more times in the next few days and got the same message. I had known that our little Eden was doomed to crumble eventually, but I hadn't expected it to end so suddenly or mysteriously. I sat in my apartment trying to study, watching clumsy transvestite prostitutes give pleasureless blowjobs to Johns no more than a paycheck from homelessness in the parking lot beneath my windows and felt pretty shitty. Everything was turning New Wave; it was suddenly the slick, New Romantic '80s. I wasn't cool enough for Lilith's crowd and I was still pretty much a freak out at the university with my self-inflicted haircuts, thrift-store clothes, and radical politics. I was reading a lot in those days and listening mostly to Crass.

Partly out of loneliness and partly for nostalgia's sake, I guess, I ended up going back to work at the same bookstore the next summer. I started work the very day after I'd only stopped in to say hello to my old manager. I pretended that it was fate that they'd asked me—even begged me—to come back. Probably I had courted it, subconsciously—had it in the back of mind when I'd "just stopped by to say hello." Both the manager and the boss had been awfully glad to see me; the two junkies I'd worked with the year before had ripped the store off blind after I'd gone, when they'd been left alone nights to run the place.

It was a while before I ran into Lilith again. Someone told me that she hadn't been hanging out in North Beach, that she'd just disappeared a couple of months before. Courtney, too, was long gone—she'd moved to Minneapolis, I'd heard. I'd already stopped looking for either of them, so it caught me by surprise when I saw Lilith sitting at the counter of the Arab hamburger stand on Broadway, next to the Vietnamese noodle place where I was heading to spend my dinner break one rainy Tuesday night.

Lilith forced a smile when she saw me, but she didn't look happy at all. I went in and sat down next to her at the counter and asked how she was doing. Of course the whole thing was really about "why did you disappear?" But we meandered around through some meaningless conversation without getting to it. Somehow I just couldn't be pissed-off or confrontational; I didn't actually feel angry with her anymore. Besides that, she looked pretty bad there under the fluorescent lights, tired and worn out, her hair oily and shrunken. I would have felt like I was picking on her or something. Even her roaring, confident voice had grown breathy and ashamed.

She started telling me how horrible her life had been that winter and I forgot all about my problems with her. She'd become a total junkie, she said, and had lost everything. She'd been thrown out of her apartment because she'd gone down to the corner with a friend who was buying. "That was even before I was shooting. But everyone's so afraid of junkies, you know. My roommates threw all my stuff out on the street, and, since it was the Fillmore, heart of the fucking Western Addition, there wasn't anything left by the time I got home. Home, yeah—well, it wasn't home anymore, was it?"

She'd lived here and there, with a girlfriend who was shooting, and they'd shot together. "We were always together and I started fucking up real bad and I got fired from my job." Then she'd been raped. "I was walking alone way down South of Market, going to the Hotel Utah to see a band, and these three sailors pushed me into a van. It was funny, one guy was scared shitless and could hardly get it up and kept apologizing, but this other one was a total asshole and kept trying to shove things in my mouth and shit. Anyway, I've only been with women since then."

She was hitting the streets of North Beach for the first time in a while, but she didn't say where she was coming from—seems like it must have been out of jail or a detox of some sort. She didn't have much money and had taken a room at the biggest flophouse, the one on Columbus Avenue, across from Francis Ford Coppola's copper-domed wedge-like office building that leans precariously over everything on the Columbus slope, marking the triangular meeting place of Chinatown, Telegraph Hill, and the Financial District: the beacon at the trivium.

I don't know—talking to me seemed to cheer Lilith up a little. I don't think she'd had much in the way of prospects that evening before I'd come along. I was willing to help her and told her she should save her money, ditch the hotel, and come stay with me as I had plenty of room. I hadn't been able to keep my studio over the school year, 'cause it cost too much, but now I was sharing a pretty big apartment on top of Nob Hill with my old friend James from Walnut Creek, he of the orange Capri who had thought that Dead Kennedys was the wittiest band name ever and who'd been driving the night I'd first talked with Lilith at the Mab. The building where we lived had once been elegant but was now falling in around our ears—it was owned by one of Chinatown's most notorious slumlords. It *was* up on top of Nob Hill though, at the corner of Clay and Leavenworth, on a lovely block with wide sidewalks, trees, better-kempt Victorians than ours, and a great view down the steep slope of Clay Street and over toward the spires of Cathedral Hill. We lived in the apartment below the bass player in Toiling Midgets, I told her, and I'd even gotten to where I kind of liked to hear him practicing. Still, it was creepy to see Ricky Williams wandering around the halls of our building sometimes, stoned out of his mind, intense as hell as always.

Lilith thanked me but didn't want to come stay at my place. She might have been a little afraid that I'd expect her to fuck me or whatever, but I didn't. Besides, she'd already paid for her room at the hotel and seemed to want to do things on her own. That was cool, and, as we talked, she cheered up and started going on about bands and how she was gonna finally get one together as soon as she got some kind of a job and a real place to stay and stuff. She was acting like her old self again, and I started feeling pretty good about seeing her, totally forgetting about asking her why she'd vanished out of my life so suddenly the year before, imagining it had been because of our distance back then, her crazy life of sex and drugs and rock 'n' roll not mixing with my trying to get through school. I was getting pretty insufferably enlightened back then, after all, and I was probably a drag to be around. My major was International Relations and, as I went on with it, I was getting more and more politicized, listening to my new heroes Crass all the time (who Lilith hated) and drawing up plans for the Anarchist International, for the eventual cultural revolution.

Looking at the clock above the counter of the hamburger stand, I told Lilith that I had to get back to work, and she said that she was going over to Oakland to get some of her stuff at Michael's. (Michael was her legendary boyfriend, who she'd been with on and off for years, way before she'd met me, and I guess after me as well, as she obviously had left what remained of her possessions at his place.) She told me she'd come by the bookstore when she got back to the city and that we'd go out for a drink to celebrate our reunion or something when I got off work at midnight. Lilith was all smiles as she went off down Columbus Avenue, turning to wave at me, and I was happy and it was pleasantly nostalgic to have seen her again.

Later that night Lilith came running into the bookstore crying and desperate. She had a black eye and was all bruised up. When she saw me she collapsed into my arms and told me that Michael had beaten her up because she owed him money and that she was lucky he hadn't killed her. I was seriously pissed off at the motherfucker and felt bad for Lilith, who seemed to me to be right on the edge, trying to get her life together again after all the shit that had happened to her.

"What a fucking asshole," I said, taking her up to the back room and sitting her down on the sofa, leaving Jeff, my co-worker at the bookshop, in command of the store. "What's fucking wrong with that guy?"

She cried for a while and I held her and we rocked back and forth on the old sofa where we use to make love and finally she said, "I don't know why I came here, to you. You've got even more reason to hate me than he does."

"No I don't, Lilith. I don't care anymore that you walked out on me. I know that I'm not for you, that we have two totally different lives."

"No, that's not what I was talking about. It's *why* I walked out on you that you don't know."

"What do you mean?"

Amazingly she stared me down, stopping for a second before saying it as if to build a wall around us. "It's because I was pregnant, and I knew you'd want me to have the baby and I couldn't go through with it. I had an abortion and I was so fucked up... It took all the money I'd saved up from working at Quicksilver. And then, when I got thrown out of my apartment, I just went on, full speed ahead, doing all the drugs I could get my hands on. I mean, fuck it, what am I gonna do, work in a fucking café for the rest of my life putting the foam on people's cappuccinos? Fuck that! I wanna do something real!"

Although the whole speech was more recited than said, and seemed kinda prepared beforehand, it floored me. I was disconcerted about it without really knowing what it was that I was feeling exactly. I mean, the bottom dropped out of my stomach and I got this sensation that I always get, that my whole life's decided far away from me by other people and that I have so little to do with it I might as well not even be there most of the time.

"Hey, that's not fair—I would have been there to help you out."

"No, you wouldn't have. You were totally busy with your school work and I didn't want to have to deal with you, 'cause I knew you'd want me to have the baby but I'd have been completely destroyed by it. Well, I sort of wanted it a little too, and I was afraid you'd talk me into it. But, come on, how am I gonna have a kid?"

Lilith had always told me that she was sterile and not to worry about birth control and we'd never used anything ever. I stood there, stunned, thinking about that.

"You know, like I was gonna ruin your life too. I mean, you've got things you wanna do, school and stuff." She hugged me 'cause she could see I was going away into myself, just sitting there staring, totally struck dumb. "But it would have been a smart little thing, huh? It would have been fucking smart, that's for sure."

I looked into her dark eyes and they were right there, waiting for me like they'd always been, deep and enveloping, and I fell into them happily. I started bawling, of course, and I thought that she was right, that I would have wanted her to have the baby. "How did you know I would have wanted to keep it?"

Lilith was always the center of attention and she talked so much you would have thought she was oblivious to everyone around her, but she wasn't. She laughed and said, "I know you, that's all."

Later, when my friends all assured me that she'd only told me this to get me to take care of her so she could rip me off 'cause she was a fucking junkie, I had to wonder if this wasn't Lilith's coup de grâce, if I wasn't a stupid sucker who believed everything she ever said, even when she told me what I was feeling inside myself. In my heart, though, I still want to imagine that everything she told me was true and that she never lied. Of course, it'd be a lot easier on me to decide she was lying then, that I never fathered a child, that she was using me, and that the only thing I did wrong was to trust her.

I went back to the counter and closed the bookstore at midnight while Lilith sat in the back room reading. We went out into the night and I bought her a bottle and she took me to her hotel room where the clerk was a total asshole about the key and more or less assumed I was a trick Lilith was turning. We finally got to her room and she took off her sweater and there was this ugly scar running across her throat. "What's that?" I asked, incredulous.

"Oh, you haven't seen it yet, I forgot. I tried to hang myself a couple months ago. Michael found me and cut me down. I was super fucking depressed. I tried it with heroin once too. I was unconscious, alone in my apartment for about a week, I think, but I didn't die. I'm practically indestructible, don't you think?" She was already into the bottle, her hand shaking as she poured out shots.

The little room was the definition of depressing; not artfully tattered or romantically kitsch like the lonely hotel rooms in movies, but so empty and worn that you could feel the thousands of well-meaning people who'd gotten stuck there, their lives having hit rock bottom. You could smell them, each and every one.

I asked Lilith again if she wanted to come to my place. That flophouse hotel room had the same feeling as an old cafeteria, a hospital, or an old folks' home, and I was afraid to let her spend the night there alone, drunk and beaten up.

There was a pile of cigarette butts on the table and Lilith started opening them up, shoving the unburned tobacco guts into a leaf of rolling paper to make herself another smoke, and told me again that she'd be okay, that she liked being alone these days. I helped her get her clothes off and to climb into bed, checked out her bruises and saw that she didn't have any cuts or broken bones or anything. I kissed her goodnight, shut out the light and went home, taking my long nightly walk out of the lights and bustle of touristy North Beach up over the hill on Clay Street, breathless and weary.

A couple of days later, her money almost gone, Lilith did finally give in, pack her only bag, and come to stay at my place. James pretended not to mind, but I think he was a little suspicious, considering the state Lilith was in.

Things were okay for a while. Lilith was at least off the streets and I gave her a little money every so often, so she had some time to look for a job and to get herself together. I was trying not to put a lot of pressure on her. I wanted Lilith to know that somebody cared about her enough to help her out.

We had some fun too. One night the Dead Kennedys were playing at Bill Graham's redone Fillmore West, right next door to the old Temple Beautiful. The Temple had been closed for a long time, had actually been Jim Jones's headquarters for a while. Once I'd even heard some people had rented the place and were trying to get orgies going there, but that they couldn't get any women to come. Maybe all that was before it became the New Wave a Go-Go. Who can follow the chronology of gossip?

We rushed over to Market Street after I got off work and grabbed a 38 bus out Geary, but we arrived at the Fillmore pretty late and they weren't letting anyone in anymore 'cause it was packed full to the rafters. It was amazing how popular the Kennedys had become now that they were pretty much irrelevant. We stood around outside for a while, hoping that the bouncers would relent and let us go in when some people cleared out, but the DKs were on by then and nobody was leaving.

Lilith took me around the corner then and said, "Let's try to get in through the old Temple Beautiful. You used to be able to get inside there pretty easily. Maybe we can find a way into the Fillmore from that side."

"Really? I'd love to see it again. It's been years since I've been in there—I used to love that place. I sort of feel like I grew up there."

She led me around through the vacant lot in back of the Temple and, sure enough, the back door was closed but easily pushed open. We were a little hesitant to step inside at first as it was a totally black emptiness beyond the doorframe—there wasn't any light at all. We took hold of each other's hands, though, and started groping our way along the walls until we found some steps.

"Do you think this goes up to the temple itself or to some offices or something in the back?"

"I've been in here before and I sort of remember that these stairs lead to a door that comes out alongside the altar at one floor, and then they go up to some other rooms behind the altar after that."

"When were you in here?"

"It's a shooting gallery sometimes. You lead the way, go on, and I'll feel for the door when we get to the landing."

"Orpheus and Eurydice," I squeezed her hand. "Up we go."

It was amazing when we found the landing. You could hear the thudding bass and drums from the Kennedys echoing all through the empty old synagogue, through its broken windows. Then, when Lilith pushed the door aside, the space opened up huge in front of us, filled with glare from the floodlights above the fire escape side of the Fillmore. It was hot and overcrowded over there and lots of people were hanging out and smoking on the long, balcony-like fire escape, trying to get some air and still be able to say that they had been to the Kennedys' show.

We walked out into the enormous dance floor in the middle of the Temple, which was just as I remembered it, except dusty and shadowy now rather than smoky and nightclub dark. Without people it felt even more vast, indifferent and blurred by the memories I had of being in that space with big crowds and loud music. All of the windows and some of the pews were busted, broken up, shit written on them and the walls, and there were places where people had lit fires to keep warm in the wintertime. As a matter of fact, the whole thing burned to the ground a few years later, one night when I was at the Hotel Utah seeing an American Music Club show.

Lilith and I walked around a little, talking about the old days, getting noticed by the punks on the long fire escape next door, who started cheering us on to climb out the windows and come over to their side of the forbidding barbed-wire fence that divided the two properties. (It was a little like the no-man's land between the trenches in a WWI movie.) We found an easy place to get out of the Temple, but it was quite a bit harder to get over the fence. We did it though, to the chanting and applause of our audience, who then gave us an arm up onto the fire escape, and we went casually inside the Fillmore to see the Kennedys.

We heard only two or three songs before the show ended and it was still like the best concert I've ever been to in my life—the force of nostalgia and loyalty, I suppose. Lilith found some of her friends who told us about an all-night party South of Market, so we ended up going down there afterward.

When we got home, drunk and exhausted, we both fell into bed right away—it was a big double bed and Lilith didn't seem to mind sharing it and having me nearby at night. We got a little cuddly, but I remembered that she'd been raped and didn't want to push anything. She fell asleep then, pretty quickly, but I was cranked enough about the whole evening not to be able to settle down. Time seemed to be dragging on endlessly as I lay there not sleepy at all. I must have, finally, nodded off, but not very deeply; it was more like a trance of some sort, filled with weird dreams.

And the next thing I knew we were making love. I sort of faded awake somewhere in the middle of it. And it was like it had always been, Lilith with her back to me, only tonight she lay facedown on the bed and was pulling me up on top of her. It was too late to stop by the time I was actually aware of what was happening, but I got kind of self-conscious as it went on and I came more and more to myself, and I regretted the whole thing before it was over.

The next morning, after we'd been up for a while, Lilith asked me if we'd had sex the night before. "I think so," I said.

"I thought so too." She kissed me, I guess to sort of tell me it was okay. Still, I felt bad about it, like I'd forced her, or manipulated her, like I'd made her pay her keep or something—although the whole thing had seemed pretty spontaneous on both of our parts. Consciously or not, I still believe I only wanted to fuck her because I loved her. I know I only let her stay with me 'cause I wanted to help her get back on her feet, and that's all.

But Lilith couldn't seem to make it in the straight world anymore. She got a job for a while in a croissant and coffee place in the Financial District, but she came home hyped up and ranting one afternoon, sick of the businessmen who were always treating her like shit or propositioning her—offering her money too.

"Fuck it, I'd rather go out and walk the streets!" She took off her jeans, crying and banging around the bedroom recklessly. "What am I gonna do, put up with all this fucking shit for minimum wage for the rest of my stupid life?" She yanked a wrinkled-up Catholic schoolgirl skirt out of her bag and sat down on the bed, trying to pull a pair of torn fishnet stockings up her legs.

I eventually talked her out of it, when she had calmed down some, and we went out and had dinner somewhere.

I figured that she was shooting again when I gave her a hundred dollar bill one morning (I never kept my money in banks, and since I had access to a cash register at work, it was easiest to store my savings in hundreds). It was supposed to keep her going for a couple of weeks while she looked for another job, but she came home that very evening crying, telling me she'd accidentally put the bill through the false pocket in the overcoat of mine that she was borrowing. "It must have fallen on the ground somewhere between here and the Caffe Trieste," she claimed. "I walked back and forth between here and there all afternoon looking for it."

What could I do but believe her, or pretend to believe her, and give her another chance—and another hundred?

One night I stepped on something on my bedroom floor, which turned out to be her needle. There it was, sticking into my heel. I sighed, pulled it out and gave it back to her. I mean, I was pissed to see it, but what was I going to do? I'm not at all the type to lay down ultimatums.

And then, a few weeks later, James came to me, calm but serious. A bunch of his autographed CDs had disappeared. Lilith swore over and over again that she hadn't taken them. I broke down and cried, begging her to cop to taking them and to tell me the truth so that I could go out and try to buy them back from whomever she'd sold them to. I had to kick her out of the apartment anyway; I'd already told James that I would, so what difference did it make to her if she admitted to stealing the CDs or not? At least she could have helped me to get my friend's stuff back.

I mostly wanted her to tell me the truth so that I could feel like she trusted me at least that much, after everything I'd done for her. But she never did. We cried and cried, holding each other, knowing that this was going to be the end of everything that'd passed between us. I couldn't trust her anymore, so she couldn't get anything more out of me. I didn't think then that either of us would ever have anything to do with the other after she left the apartment.

James found a couple of the CDs at a used-record store on Polk Street a week or so later, and the guy at the counter described Lilith perfectly as the seller.

She went back to the North Beach flophouses after we threw her out, the Golden Eagle on Broadway this time, and got a job working the door of the Condor Club, underneath Courtney's old apartment. Her ex-best friend and rival was long gone by then though, had even made a movie and was soon to marry the hottest singer-songwriter on the punk revival scene that was just beginning to hit it big. Courtney was probably a fucking millionairess by now.

Lilith told me that she'd cut a deal with the owner of the Condor, that she only had to work the door as a barker, wearing a silly late-nineteenth-century bordello-type costume and banging on a tambourine. He'd told her she didn't have to strip unless she wanted to. I was pretty skeptical, but glad that she had some kind of a job and wasn't walking the streets. I thought Lilith might not do so many drugs, too, if she had to pay for them herself and if her life were a little less miserable than it had been. It was weird though, walking past her on my dinner break from work and saying "hi" while she stood there winking and flirting with the sailors and businessmen that she so despised.

She came into the bookstore one afternoon, totally high, to show me a letter: Some of the translations she'd done of the Roman poet Catullus had been published in a review. She'd been a Classics major in college back East, where she was from originally, before dropping out and coming to San Francisco to start that band that she'd never been able to get going.

The little journal hadn't paid her a lot, but enough for a fix, I guess. It was sad because I knew she didn't write much anymore, with all the shit happening in her life, and she'd shown me great poems and song lyrics when we'd been together before. I guess she'd lost most of her notebooks along the way. But she didn't complain: It was probably too depressing to think about.

Another time she came running into the store crying because her boss at the Condor had tried to force her to get up on stage and strip and she'd finally been fired for refusing and telling him off. We went upstairs and sat on the couch and I tried to encourage her to get away from North Beach and the whole rotten scene there. It was bad in those days; there weren't any clubs or artists or writers much anymore, just junkies, tourists, and sailors during Fleet Week.

She told me that she had fallen heavily for a woman at a party the weekend before, a beautiful lesbian she described as "a long cool drink of water," who worked as a dominatrix. "She took me home with her, and I was so flattered," she said.

"Well, go for it, Lilith," I told her. "You need a change of scenery. You're mired in this shit around North Beach. Maybe she'll let you stay with her while you get a fresh start. Where does she live?"

"Over in Oakland."

"Go ahead and give her a call. Use our phone."

For the next few months Lilith was, as they say, out of sight and out of mind. I'd more or less finished school, leaving one course incomplete that I'd never make up, and was now working at the bookstore full-time, not sure what to do with the rest of my life, when a middle-aged man I'd never seen before walked in one afternoon and asked for me by name.

He told me he was looking for Lilith, using her real name. "I guess she calls herself 'Lilith.' I'm her father. I'm here to take her home. You've got to help me find her."

I didn't know what the hell to tell him—that I'd had to kick her out of my place for stealing from my roommate? That she was maybe living in Oakland with a professional dominatrix? That she was a notorious junkie by now with a reputation all over North Beach for ripping off her friends? (Missy, one of the women who'd worked at the bookstore that first summer I was there, had told me, even after her beating, that Lilith's boyfriend Michael was a sweetheart compared to her.)

Well, I ended up stuttering out the logistical facts: that I hadn't seen her for a couple of months, and that she might have been living somewhere in Oakland. I gave him the names of all of the flophouses in North Beach and told him to ask around at the Condor Club—where she'd only worked as a barker, I assured him, *not* as a stripper.

He went away disappointed, I think, that Lilith wasn't still staying at my place, but hopeful that he'd be able to track her down, perhaps enjoying the detective work.

A couple of weeks later, Lilith herself charged into the bookstore, all cranked up and high. She grabbed me, talking a mile a minute, happy and loud, dragging me off toward the stairs to the back room, to tell me good-bye, she said.

"Hey, your dad's been in here looking for you, you know."

"Yeah, I know. He's out in the car waiting for me right now. But I wanted to stop in and tell you good-bye. He's taking me back to Connecticut."

When she got me to the door of the back room where our old couch was, she couldn't get in. The boss had locked it up when he'd gone home that afternoon and I didn't have a key. The boss didn't trust anybody anymore. Lilith pounded on the door, cursing, scaring me with her sudden strength and fury.

Then she turned to me, holding me close, saying, "I wanted to say good-bye and give you a present for helping me so much."

She pulled me down onto the carpeted floor of the landing and unzipped my pants.

"Come on, Lilith, what are you doing?"

"Giving you a going-away present."

She pulled my cock out, bent over and put it in her mouth. I was actually kind of frightened and had let her storm through the store and lead me back here because I didn't know what else to do with her, and had been embarrassed by the scene she'd made in front of all the customers. I didn't know how to deal with people on drugs. Now I was petrified, lying there helplessly underneath her, totally freaked out and kinda weirdly touched too; it was the most affection she'd shown me since I'd had to kick her out of my apartment.

But I couldn't deal with it. I tried to pull her off of me. "Lilith, you don't owe me anything. Come on, it was never like that between us."

I saw the tracks on her arms, when I tried to lift her up by them, all the scabs and bruises. "Oh, Lilith," I said pitifully, holding on to her, "look at you." She stared up at me like a zombie, I thought, with the dark circles under her eyes, her tangled black curls, and her gaze eerily far away.

"Oh, that's nothing. I've been a good girl lately." She giggled then, slipping her panties off, out from under her skirt, and sitting on me, painfully.

I winced and she said, "I know it's dry, but I just don't have the patience to give a blowjob right now."

All I remember feeling by this point was numb fear and sorrow for Lilith, for my lonely fucking self, for the whole miserable world. I was in shock. I kept thinking that I didn't want this, but I couldn't seem to get out from under her. I felt sorry for Lilith but I loved her too and it did feel like some kind of intense last moment between us and I wanted her love still. It all happened so quickly and unexpectedly and was so intense that I felt like I didn't have any time to react at all. I couldn't make any sense out of what was happening to me.

Then I just came. I was thinking about our baby, about her having been pregnant before, so I managed to pull myself out from under her.

"No, Sam," she said, grabbing my dick and pulling it back toward her as the cum dropped onto the filthy, old carpet.

"What? Did you want to get pregnant again? That's about the last thing you need right now. That's what totally fucked you up before."

She sat back against the wall then and finally started to calm down. We said our good-byes quietly, promised to write, and she went out onto Columbus Avenue and I never saw or heard from her again.

But I do see a lot of Courtney these days. I see her videos on MTV and I hear her songs everywhere. They always make me think of Lilith, of course, and I wonder if her father really was outside the bookstore that day, waiting for her in the car. It doesn't seem very likely to me now.

A couple of years later I caught a fever while traveling in Italy. I was in Mantua, which was basically built in the middle of a swamp, and I caught what Cellini, in his *Autobiography*, calls the *"Guata."* It's a kind of swamp fever you get from mosquitoes that's particular to the city. It got so bad that they let me stay in bed all day long in the youth hostel. The woman who ran the place kindly took my money, went out and bought me lots of aspirin and eventually some antibiotics.

During the hot summer afternoons the cleaning lady would come in, scrub the floors, open the windows to let out the ammonia smell, and close the green shutters up tight to keep the sunlight out. Lying there in the humid, summer heat and the artificial darkness, I went in and out of sleep and had fever dreams. In one of them Lilith and I were back on that landing in the bookstore and she was saying, "I only wanted to give you a present." She was sitting on top of me and in the dream I suddenly knew that it was AIDS that she'd wanted to give me and that I was dying now, here in Mantua, where Virgil had been born, the city founded by the sorceress Manto, who'd cursed her own people by choosing this godforsaken swamp as the site for their city.

When I got better I realized it had only been a dream, probably born of the guilt I felt for not being able to save Lilith from herself, but I went and got tested all the same, 'cause it made me nervous to think about it. I guess I wouldn't have blamed Lilith for wanting me to die with her. And that was probably because I sort of felt like I deserved to share her fate, or wanted to somehow—'cause that's the romantic way to look at it. When I got the results in the mail I sat down and asked Lilith, wherever she was, to forgive me. I'd done whatever I'd done because I loved her and because I hadn't known any better in those days. The test was negative.

I hear Courtney's songs on the radio now and they're quite good, I think, and I wonder if Lilith hears them or if she's dead or what. Courtney's famous husband is dead: heroin again being the scapegoat for our whole generation's implosion. I wonder if Lilith likes Courtney's songs, or if she's cringing every time she turns on the radio. And I wonder what Lilith's songs would have sounded like if she'd ever gotten that band together and been able to sing them. And of course our baby, if it ever really did exist, what kind of a person would it have grown up to be? I can't even imagine now, and it's all supposed to have happened to me.

4: A DREAM

I must have had a friend. There must have been someone brave enough to hold my hand. Maybe I've said too much; I remember his disinterested and unctuous green eyes looking off, through the smoke coming from the cigarette he always held in front of his face. I can still picture him, burning himself out on speed, looking for trouble, a pack of Export A's in his pocket.

Now I remember the dream — it was about the woman who came between us. Naked in an open horizontal freezer like we used to have in the garage when I was a kid, her hair knotted up in an ice-water bath. She's looking at me through the liquid and chunks of ice without much of an expression and I wonder how she can stare at me so calmly 'cause I can't keep my eyes open under water — it hurts. I reach down into the numbing bathwater and put my hands around her throat, holding her still. I'm listening to the clacking of the ice cubes as she sways in the clear, frosty sludge, like someone turning to get comfortable in bed. Still looking me in the eyes, she remarks casually, "This is stupid." I agree, we laugh about it, and I let her up.

I'm looking down into the empty freezer now—no one is looking back at me, and I am alone. Our love has become a gift pulled out of my hands, a rhythm broken. I wasn't invited to the most important event of my young life.

TROUBLED RECOGNITIONS

Lee puts the round key into the bike lock, unhooks it, draws the lock out of its resting place—hanging from the back of the moped by the short sissy bar—and slides it through the spokes of the front wheel and around a pole of the painter's scaffolding. The moped belongs to his girlfriend Betty; he should have returned it to her a while ago. After locking the bike to the steel pole, he reaches over the seat and turns off the gas flow. Betty never remembers to do that, and he remembers only sometimes.

Finished with the chore, Lee raises his head, his face splashed a spectral white from the streetlights along Geary Street, and looks up at the scaffolding; the metal poles are humming softly in the cold wind that's blowing in off of the ocean, down through the avenues of the Sunset and Richmond districts, up over Cathedral Hill, and is now swirling around down here in the Polk Street gulch. The metal frames of the scaffolding are crosshatched with wooden planks and the dusty framework stands up against the façade of the building next door to the bar where Lee is meeting the rest of the band. The boards are worn, splintered, spotted with drippings of white paint. It reminds him of the scaffolding that had stood in front of the house where he and Betty had lived together. All that fall their landlord—who'd moved into the basement flat of the building, nullifying the rent control—had been repairing their building out in the Western Addition. When he'd finished he raised their rent and they'd had to move.

Walking toward the bar now, the Edinburgh Castle, Lee looks up the street for his friends. They're all coming in Adrian's car and it'll take 'em a while to find a parking space. Lee has come on ahead to get the fish and chips ordered before the place stops serving food, at ten.

He pushes the swinging doors and goes in, turns the corner skirting the tiny Scottish souvenir shop, and walks into the bar proper. The space is bigger inside than you'd imagine from looking at the door on the street, and dark—thick wooden booths line the wall opposite the bar itself, with a wide-open space down the center of the room between the bar on the one side and the booths on the other. The ceiling is high and there are balconies running along the two walls lengthwise, one roofing the bar, the other above the booths along the facing wall. Winston the Green parrot sits silently on his perch in his cage at the end of the bar, near the television, which plays without sound in the corner.

Lee walks past the bar and up to the raised platform against the back wall, a sort of mezzanine between the end of the bar and the stairs to the balconies. He sits at the big round table up there with his back against the wall. Phony spears and shields are draped about the wall behind him. The shield Lee likes best—a perching tiger in one of its corners—is spotlighted above his head.

The room feels warm after facing the wind head on while riding uphill from the Tenderloin. That comforting but stale bar smell cuddles up around Lee, thickly in the dim light. Waiting, he gets lost in his thoughts. All that last semester he'd been studying Eastern philosophy and art, trying to find some sense of balance and symmetry in a world he had always seen as hopelessly skewed, corrupt, competitive, and unfair.

The young waiter—as opposed to one of the much older bartenders—comes up, wearing a tartan vest, sporting a tidy mustache and newly cut, feathered hair. Jesus, Lee thinks, I thought the '70s were over. He orders four fish and chip suppers for the band and a pint of Bass Ale for himself. The bar begins to feel lighter, slowly, as his eyes adjust and he drinks his beer. He starts checking out the people sitting at the other tables, couples mostly, eating and chatting, the lonelier, heavy drinking customers lined up along the bar.

A few moments later the rest of the band strolls in. Adrian, the guitarist, rigid and short, walking behind the others as they cross the room, sees Lee first. He smirks his wide, beautiful smile at Lee, nods, and leads Devin, the singer, and Johnny, the bass player, up to where Lee sits. Adrian crosses in and out of the spots of electric light toward the thick monastic table, his slow, calculated, and carefully executed strides nearly feminine, his stocky legs clad in tight dark-green jeans. Adrian's sharkskin jacket shines from black to emerald when the light hits it. He carries Lee's white evening jacket over his bent forearm.

"Faustus," he says, springing up the wooden steps, flourishing the jacket in the air and dropping it into Lee's lap.

"Mephistopheles," Lee chuckles.

"I forgot to give you your coat back at rehearsal."

"Thanks."

"Did you order food for all of us?" Devin asks.

"Only food. I didn't know what kind of beer you'd want."

"Looks like a fun place," says Johnny, the bassist, a tall Chinese kid wearing red-tinted prescription glasses, nodding his head and settling his lanky limbs into a chair on Lee's left, across from Adrian. As he leans back, Johnny's face tilts into a beam of light and Lee sees the outline of his warm eyes, his large, enthusiastic grin, and the scars on his ruddy cheeks from a serious bout with acne during adolescence. He wears a perfectly sculpted black flattop haircut, a grand burgundy-tinted cowlick sticking up out of it, accenting his high forehead.

With a quick, fluid motion, Devin, the singer, lights his first cigarette, his eyes roving carefully around the room from behind his clear, tortoise-shell glasses. His head looks very round against the light on the wall behind him except for his pointy chin, unshaven and stubbly. His short, tightly curled hair and clothes are black. "I need a drink," he says, smiling suddenly—like he always does—as if he were ashamed because he had noticed you there looking at him, or as if saying something were some sort of mistake for which he needed to apologize.

Adrian lights a cigarette as well, looking impishly at his three band mates, his eyes blue, green, and lively.

The waiter comes back, wondering what everyone wants to drink. "Bass, a pint," Adrian says, lowering his cigarette to the ashtray by laying his arm flat against the table. He gives the cigarette a quick tap to its underside with his thumb and the ashes scatter into the air and settle into the ashtray's amber circle of glass.

"Yeah, the same," Devin says, his eyes flowing around the table, his voice deep, sad in a resigned but also awkward way, as if it were always looking for something, going somewhere.

"What's that you're drinking, Bass too?" Johnny asks Lee, pointing at the pint in front of him.

"Yeah, it's good stuff."

"You've had it before?"

"Uh-huh," Adrian jumps in, impatiently, at once annoyed at Johnny's indecision and smug about knowing exactly what he wants.

"Uhhh," Johnny looks at Lee and shrugs. "Sure, what the hell, give me one too."

Adrian, sitting on Lee's other side, asks—after the waiter's gone and Devin and Johnny have started up a conversation of their own— "How's the sex life going?" He asks quietly, exhaling smoke over his cigarette, looking past Lee, toward the booths along the wall and the balcony above. Up there it's closed off tonight, dark, the tables empty.

"Betty and I aren't seeing each other right now."

"What happened?"

"Well, you know me, I keep trying to come up with logical solutions to all of our problems."

Adrian chuckles, running his index finger along the wood-grain pattern of the table, the lines exaggerated by wear, shaking his head.

"I know it's stupid," Lee continues, "but I actually believe that there should be some logical reasons for what we do and answers to all of our not being able to get along. Of course there aren't and all of my thinking doesn't seem to be doing us much good, but I've got to do something 'cause I'm going fucking crazy. I try to relax, as if it doesn't mean that much to me, but then..." He makes a helpless movement with his hands. "I'm being an idiot, I guess."

Lee leans forward, cupping his beer with one hand and fingering the metal keys and change in his pocket with the other. "I just don't understand how someone who's supposed to love me can treat me so coldly sometimes. I'm only trying to make things better between us. I've made lots of suggestions, but she always takes things the wrong way, as if I only say stuff to get back at her or something. I thought that maybe it would be better for us if we spent a little time apart. But she took that totally the wrong way and got mad because she wouldn't be able to go to Johnny's party, like that matters more than our relationship."

"I still think you should just get out of it."

"Sure, that's easy to say when you're looking in from the outside, when you have no direct attachment."

The waiter brings the beers and everybody reaches into their pockets and tosses bills onto the table.

"That's rough," Adrian says when the waiter's gone, "but at least you've got someone. I am, as they say, green with envy and pretty hard up at this point."

"Yeah, but it's hardly worth it. The storms totally outnumber the calms these days. Christ, you'd think we'd be able to work things out between us by now—we've been together for two whole years. She doesn't understand that sometimes I'm hurt too. She reads everything I say as anger. It's the same old argument over and over."

"Well, drink more," Devin interrupts, raising his pint glass. Adrian pours some of his ale into Lee's almost empty glass so they can make a toast. "To the great goddess of nuptial bliss!" Devin winks.

"So, what do you think of the Edinburgh Castle?" Lee asks, sitting up straight, spreading his arms out.

"Cool place," Adrian says and the others nod, Johnny smiling approvingly, Devin still gulping at his ale. "Cool" was the highest compliment Adrian ever gave; Lee had only recently begun to earn the honor.

Johnny pulls a red disposable lighter lazily out of his jeans' pocket, his bare arms bony in the half-light, black plastic bracelets jangling. He brings the flame up to a cigarette of his own. Johnny looks at the other two smokers, grins at Lee, and asks him, "So, when are you gonna start smoking?" This is a running joke. The band rehearses in a tiny L-shaped room with only one window above a porno movie theater in the Tenderloin and the other three smoke in-between songs, sometimes even while they're playing, nearly suffocating Lee every time they get together.

"Yeah," Adrian prompts, "you bum, I haven't seen you do any drugs either." Adrian's specialty is crystal meth. "You know you'd love it, you're a white boy, come on." Johnny laughs heartily at that, shaking his head.

"Probably love it too much, knowing me."

Devin leans forward, his hands making little nervous movements on the table. "You've never done speed?" Lee shakes his head no. "Any drugs?" Devin asks, his black eyes placid, reflective.

"No."

"Never done acid?" Johnny asks.

"Oh, don't do acid. It's a nasty drug," Devin advises.

"It can be real good, too," Johnny points out.

"Yeah, and just as awful if it backfires on you. No, speed's the drug—but you can get too deep into it real fast if you're not careful." Adrian nods at Lee in agreement with Devin.

"You were quite a speed freak there for a while," Johnny reminds Devin, stretching his arm across the table to get at the ashtray, flicking the red, dying embers from his cigarette.

Devin reflects, in a rapid flow of thoughts, on being a speed freak. He remembers Seattle, his military father and his disturbed mother who'd left the family when he was only seven months old. He'd come to San Francisco instead of going to college and mixed into the art school crowd, working at a gallery, painting, doing a lot of speed and being briefly out of his mind. Dealing with his wife and her pregnancy had been keeping him busy and off drugs other than pot for a while now.

Lee remembers that Betty had told him she'd been something of a speed freak back in high school, long before he'd known her—and the phrase always reminded him of her. "I was like Concord's biggest coke dealer." He hears the words in her voice and pictures her face suddenly, her wide blue eyes, hennaed hair, amber skin, her sweet, fragile smile and exaggerated cheeks, her pouty bottom lip so much bigger than the top.

"What about coke?" Lee asks.

"It's a kind of speed," Adrian informs, springing up out of his lazy slouch. "It's a good aphrodisiac. Makes you forget about responsibilities—and your inhibitions." He pushes his chair out from under him with the backs of his thighs and wanders over to the dartboard. He pulls the darts out, steps back, roots his stumpy body behind the green line, gauging the distance, squinting slightly. There are more heraldic emblems and shields on the wall beside him and a turquoise chalkboard for keeping score. A funny-looking dragon on a shield seems to preside over the game. Adrian winks at it, cradling the wooden darts in his pudgy hands.

"What's so bad about acid?" Lee asks.

"It depends on your mood." Devin considers for a moment, his arm balancing above the table, pivoting on his elbows, flowing abstractly in the darkness, then moving in rapid expression of his words, which suddenly come flooding out. "If you're going to do it, work up to it and do it when you're feeling good and with somebody you like." Lee's and Devin's eyes meet, confidentiality flowing between them, each thinking a bit of the others' thoughts, like a yin-yang.

Johnny starts laughing, "And if you go to the bathroom, when you're washing your hands afterward, whatever you do, don't look up into the mirror."

"Why? What happens?"

"You end up standing there for hours. You see all kinds of shit—things you never saw before. You spend hours studying every blemish. It's like, wow, where did that come from?"

"That's all that happens to you?" Devin smirks. Apparently his trips are more complex, darker perhaps, stranger than Johnny's.

"It's like," Johnny goes on, "when you look at something for a long enough time, it starts to distort, right? Well, when you're on acid, time slows down and a glance is like staring at something steadily for hours. It distorts all over the place."

"I definitely know that feeling," Lee jokes.

"Yeah, and then the next thing you know there's people outside knocking on the door, 'Hey, man, are you okay in there?'"

"Acid's rough," Devin says, leaning past Adrian's empty seat, his face close to Lee's, nodding patiently, rhythmically as a dripping faucet. Everything Devin does begins slow and inconclusive, then seems to tumble toward the lowest possible spot, tragically firm and resigned. He purposefully looks at Lee, satisfied—having doused the idea of LSD—leans back in his chair and glances at his watch. "Hope the food gets here soon, I've got to get rolling."

A serious expression overtakes Johnny's face and he asks Devin how his wife is getting along.

"Well, she's doing okay, I guess, you know, under the circumstances. It's kind of hard taking care of her all the time, going back and forth between here and the Sunset."

"When's she going to have the baby?"

"Well, you know, they've got her on this drug to arrest the labor, so it's kind of up to the doctor. She'll have the baby whenever he decides to take her off the drug."

"Is that why she can't move around?" Lee hasn't been with the band long enough to know all the details surrounding Devin's situation and his wife's pregnancy.

"Yeah." Devin looks deeply at his nearly dry pint glass.

"Did you guys plan this at all?" Lee does know that Devin has been separated from his wife for a while.

Devin looks up again, shrugging. "No. She went off the pill without telling me, after I'd moved out."

Johnny raises his glass. "Hey, cheer up, you guys."

"And let's have some more beer, huh?" Devin smiles all around the table.

Lee observes Adrian, still at the base line before the dartboard, wondering why he seems so removed tonight. "Probably he's sick of hearing about my romantic problems," he thinks. And Adrian's been hard up for a girlfriend for a while. Maybe they've been spending too much time together. He watches Adrian pull the darts out of the cork dartboard, turn, and stroll back to the baseline. He poses there, peering in at the round target, about to spring, his arm stiff, half-cocked, ready to throw, his attitude reckless.

"Hey, why don't you toss the caber?" Lee calls over to him.

Adrian tilts his head to the side, wrinkling his bushy eyebrows, wordlessly asking Lee what the hell he's talking about.

"The caber. On the wall. Behind you."

Adrian turns and admires the caber hung at an angle, parallel to the rise of the stairs going up to the balcony above the bar. His attention captured, Adrian steps closer to the long wooden log and examines the three framed, black-and-white photos demonstrating how to toss the miniature telephone pole. The first picture shows a seemingly feminine figure straining, legs bent in a posture that makes it look as if she's struggling just to hold the darned thing up. The second one clearly shows the figure to be a man, now trying to get the caber off of his chest and aloft. Lee thinks this thrower looks disappointed, as if he knows he'll never get the thing into the air. Adrian stands before the third photo, which shows the log in full flight, the tosser's back to the camera; face turned away, arms outstretched behind him, as if he were grabbing at the ascending cabor, trying to pull it back into his hands.

"Let's play darts," Lee suggests, reaching to take the darts from Adrian's hands—but, at that very same moment, the waiter brings the fish and chips and they sit back down to eat, ordering another round of beer, Lee and Devin substituting Guinness for Bass.

"They used to have Watneys on tap here, but they don't anymore."

"Watneys? I've never heard of that either. Is it good?" Johnny wants to know.

Devin nods and Lee says, "It's the best—the only beer that matters."

"Sounds good. Do you think they have it in bottles?"

"Might."

"Let's go see," says Johnny, laying a hand on Devin's shoulder, "before he brings the next round." Devin nods, and they go over to the bar to investigate.

"So, Lee," Adrian says, munching, "you going to submit any of your lyrics to this band?"

"I'm not sure. I don't know if I'd feel comfortable letting other people sing the stuff I write. I'm kinda happy only to be a drummer for a change and not to have to face an audience with nothing to protect me but a microphone."

"Devin won't mind if you sing a couple songs, I'm sure."

"Yeah, I guess. But I kind of like just drumming in a band for once, concentrating only on that."

They chew in silence for a minute and the jukebox starts up with "Amazing Grace" on bagpipes.

Lee rolls his eyes. "Somebody plays this every time I come here."

Adrian scoots up in his chair, out of his casual slouch and into a straight-backed pose, puffing out his cheeks in imitation of a bagpipe player. He always mimes along with the records he plays for Lee when they sit around his room getting drunk, and imitates people they know when telling stories about them.

Johnny and Devin come back empty-handed. "They don't have it anymore at all."

"Too bad, but maybe you wouldn't have liked it anyway. It's one of those British beers that's supposed to be served at room temperature."

After they've eaten most of the food, Johnny says, "Seems like we played pretty well tonight." He always talks about things after the fact, as if to confirm for himself that they had actually happened, or to make sure he'd interpreted the events the same way as everybody else. Devin and Lee nod in assent. Adrian goes on eating.

"The jamming was great." Lee loves improvising with Adrian on guitar; it's the most fun he's ever had playing music. Adrian has some kind of instinctual feel for rhythm that impresses him. It's like they're communicating in the same way, the same language, when they're jamming. And it's not only a bunch of clichés strung together, like what most guitarists do when they're just noodling.

It isn't all that great for Adrian though; he plays with a lot of people, his whole life being channeled into music. Still, he likes Lee, and it's okay when they play together. They spend a lot of their evenings hanging out these days, drinking and cruising around San Francisco in the deserted early morning hours in Adrian's clunky old Chevy Bonneville. They drive at night because Adrian has no license and the car is on loan from a friend. Usually they're sneaking to the café in the Richmond where Adrian sometimes works, near the house he grew up in, where his mom still lives, to steal cases of beer and bring them back to his makeshift Tenderloin apartment.

"What about the name?" Johnny asks, returning to a discussion they'd had earlier. The band had been called Troubled Recognitions (partially in homage to William Gaddis) for a while, even before Lee and Johnny had joined, and they liked it mostly in its shortened form, the Troubled Wrecks, but Johnny has been brainstorming and is now lobbying for a new name. "I love Kangaroo Court."

Devin shakes his head, laughing in short, choppy breaths. Adrian pays no visible attention. It had been Devin who had vetoed the new name at tonight's rehearsal.

"You really don't like it?"

"No, I don't. Sorry, Johnny, but it's too... absurd or something."

"Oh, well," Johnny shrugs. Then, turning to Lee he says, "I wish we could play at my party, but there isn't enough room in our flat." Johnny is planning a going-away party for Mary, his girlfriend, who'll be heading home to Scotland in a few weeks. Having said that, Johnny's thoughts immediately darken. He doesn't want Mary to go, but her visa is expiring and she doesn't want to be deported 'cause it's a lot harder to come back into the U.S. once you get deported. Besides, she needs to get back to school in London. Johnny's trying not to think about it now—there'll be plenty of time to think about it after she's gone.

"And we're not half rehearsed enough to play a show," Adrian adds. He's right: They haven't all been playing together long enough to get through an entire set competently.

Lee reaches for the vinegar. "Hey, how about this for a name?" He holds the bottle out to Adrian. "The Four Monks! We'll call our first album *Malt Vinegar* and use the label as cover art."

They all snicker. Adrian says, "Yeah, but Johnny blows it." Adrian, as usual, had been complaining to Lee and Devin earlier that day about not having been laid for so long.

"Yeah, but she'll be leaving in a few weeks and then I'll be as hard up as the rest of you guys. And you'll see, Lee will work things out with Betty soon. And Adrian, you'll jump on the first sweet young thing who looks your way."

"Hey, you guys," the waiter comes up holding a single parcel of newspaper-rolled fish and chips, "we got one too many orders tonight. I'll give it to you for half price. You up for it?"

"Yeah, I think we're up for it," Johnny says, just sarcastically enough. Devin nods, drinking, the black stout bobbing in the glass with the motion of his head; Adrian, chewing, points at the table in front of him and Lee nods. The waiter drops the fifth order down into the center of the table merrily.

The jukebox goes on with Marlene Dietrich singing "Falling in Love Again."

"Betty always plays that when we come here," Lee says. Everything seems to remind him of her, her warm smell, her soft yellowish skin, and her blue eyes narrowing at him ruefully. "So, is it good, or what?" Lee points at the dwindling food, the half-eaten fish wallowing in the amber vinegar.

The other three band members all nod and Lee is glad.

"You know, Betty and I came here on New Year's Eve, which is also the night that this place opened, so the bar was celebrating its twenty-fifth anniversary that night too. Up here on the platform they had all this free food laid out, deli and sandwich stuff. We ran out of money after a couple of drinks, so it was great to have something for free, and then this waiter started giving us drinks too, for nothing, 'cause he could tell we were broke."

"That sounds fun," Johnny says, laying a dead cigarette into the ashtray where it falls into ash, then mysteriously re-lights a second later. The jukebox flips the Marlene Dietrich single and plays the other side, "The Boys in the Back Room."

Adrian looks around the mostly empty bar and imagines it full of people. He likes Lee's girlfriend a lot, she's cool. He wonders what it would be like to sleep with her. He wonders what it would be like to sleep with a lot of women at this point.

Lee finishes his food first, so Adrian picks up the extra order and slides it in front of him. Lee unwraps the globe of newspaper guiltily, not having enough money on him to pay for it but still hungry, smelling the warmth of the yellow, battered fish as he exposes it. "We'll split it up," he says, not much wanting to.

After a while, after they've eaten all that there is to eat, and had another couple of rounds, Adrian leans back in his chair and says, "Drunk. Now what?"

9/1984
San Francisco

5: AFTERWARD

How long will it take to thaw this chill out of my hands? Poor circulation, I'm told. Ice in the bone and some wanting, always that now, over and over again, and that must be the way to love.

(Now that you've said that, remember: You've got to keep on telling the truth.)

You've got to keep yourself occupied. You can't give in. You have no freedom, no free will, not really; you've never had that luxury. Everything hurts until you're numb; you're scared of being so numb you won't care anymore—you might fall asleep. Don't fall asleep; she's talking to you. There's something you have to work out, but you just want to go to sleep. After all, it's late. But you'll never get to relax—and if she let you, it would be out of indifference and the pain of that would throw you into absolute fits. Sure, others can relax, they have that freedom; but you know you're the same as they are — sometimes you're certain of that. Remember, everything has the potential to be the most painful thing you've ever felt, but the numbness you force on yourself in its place will rob you of even that.

THE MORNING OF THE DAY

I half sat/half lay propped up on a pillow in bed looking out the bay window in the nearest corner of Betty's large bedroom in the back of her new flat—it still felt like she'd only just moved in. The old flip-clock-radio on the glossy black end table that her art-school sister had painted in the Downtown apartment that she and Betty had shared when we'd first met—about two years ago—said that it was a little after three in the morning. I hardly felt sleepy. Through the windows I'd been watching the lights of the rooms in the gray-and-white high-rise hotel down the slope of Laguna Street in Japantown go off one by one. Now there were only two or three people still awake over there.

Red warning lights were blinking at the four corners of the crest of the high-rise, well beneath the low, cloudy sky. This hovering fog, lit up by the city below, glowed above the flats and shops marching in their ordered, semi-suburban rows through the Richmond

District all the way to the ocean, a profound pinkish gray tonight, too high and thick to burn off in the morning. Tomorrow wouldn't be a pretty day.

In order to watch the lights of the high-rise I had to look over the backside of a row of modest Victorian flats lined up on Pine Street. From behind you can see that all four of the buildings have the same exact floor plan, although each has a unique façade sticking up in front of its flat roof. Their windows were closed up tight against the damp evening and it was now dark in all of the rooms into which I could see. A child lived in the back bedroom of the apartment closest to Betty's window, and I'd watched its mother put it to bed a couple of hours before, against its will, before it was really ready. It was lying quietly now in the dark, asleep, or maybe awake like me, and trying not to bother anyone.

Betty twitched and turned beside me, pushing a pocket of air out from under the comforter. I love the way she smells, her moist skin when we're in bed together, under her arms, her breasts, her thighs, and her lap around which she's curled up tonight, hugging her knees. The comforter always makes us sweat. But I felt cold suddenly, half out of the covers, still awake, staring, even though I could feel the heat coming off of Betty lying next to me.

It had only been a couple of months since we'd moved apart and I missed living with her. I'd been the one to suggest our separating for a while, but regretted it now. I'd found my friends and the bars and clubs I haunted more boring than I'd remembered them. Finally I'd pretty much given up on going out altogether. I'd pushed against the "us" of Betty and I for a long time and we always fought over things that seemed like nothing when you looked at them later. The "us" of Betty and I had withstood a lot, maybe more than it should have. It made a third thing, not exactly who we are but which we made together—a thing that never seemed to get broken by my struggling against it, or now hers.

Betty's cat, Domitia, stood up at the foot of the bed, stretched, spun around once or twice, and then curled itself into a ball, lowering its head onto its forepaws. It felt good, I thought, being the three of us all in the same bed again, but strange too, being in a different place—this apartment, which I didn't like much because of what had happened here, in this very bed, and only a few weeks before. Domitia stared at me suspiciously, as cats do.

I felt the pulse of Betty's shoulders, then, the sobbing. She hadn't been asleep, or had just woken up and was crying, thinking about it.

"Come on, Bets, it's not so bad." I pulled her toward my chest, her face hot, smelling the way it did when we made love, damp from the stifling comforter and the crying, her eyes shut tight, my dry skin skidding against her moist skin. "It'll be alright. You'll see. After tomorrow it'll all be okay." It didn't quite connect in my mind, at this hour, that tomorrow was already here—I guess because I knew we'd go to sleep after this.

"Oh, Bets. Someday we'll have a kid, you and me. And you'll hold the little thing in your arms and I'll sit there and play with it and we'll giggle." I was rocking her shoulders back and forth, her breath on my chest. I ran my hand down across her smooth stomach. "Someday we'll have one, you and me."

9/1984
San Francisco

6: THE REVELATION

You want answers? To cold—heat. A revelation! We've been trying too hard. To each other we're like sound in the air, shaking on through. We're simple, really. No, not that. We contradict. We want out. We want to fly. I began by dreaming and now look at me. We could just do our work—there are other possibilities. We're not forced to listen except to get at what we want. We don't have to be in love all the time (all the time). We could stay with these formulas or not. But why do we have to suffer for them so much, so often? It must be because we need to suffer, or want to suffer, in order to be, to change, to be other than what we were, to get out maybe, to get away from ourselves.

Is it so difficult just to be?

—Yes, it must be the most difficult thing there is, to know how to be able to be. And it isn't even the same all the time (all the time), sometimes it's easy and "Yes," and then sometimes it has to be "No."

WITH PAUL AT THE BEACH

"Kate," Paul said to me this one night while we were driving around, Alex Chilton's "Holocaust" playing on the car stereo, "why aren't we a couple? I mean, we spend so much time hanging out together, we might as well hook up, right?"

"No, Paul," I told him straight out, "I like our friendship just the way it is. I don't want to have a boyfriend right now. And I'm not so sure we'd be compatible as a couple anyway. We're pretty good friends—why complicate things?"

"Okay, okay," he said, "I get it, just friends." I know people hate being rejected and they always want to argue with your reasons for rejecting them, but, well, I was consciously working on shaping myself back then. That was part of the deal of becoming a performance artist. They were teaching us how we ourselves, how our lives, had to become works of art. So I was hyper-aware, back then, of how I was living my life through the continuum, you know, within the possibilities of time.

Because, you see, during that period when I was hanging out with Paul, I had made a vow that I wasn't going to get into a relationship with anyone for at least a year. I know how it sounds now but, at the time, decisions like that were important to me.

What I mean to say is this: Most of us live our lives open to variables, to chance, to chaos, to luck, to time itself and all of its changes. I, on the other hand, was learning from my performance art classes that I could control my life intellectually, that I could conceptually shape it. Just as an artist controls—well, you don't really control your art, but you set it in motion—the artworks that they create. You know, for a performance artist sometimes the lines get a little blurred between your life and your work.

Call it pretentious if you like, but that's what I was learning about and excited to be learning back then. These ideas were new to me and they changed me a lot, both the way I looked at art and the way I looked at my life. I made decisions regarding the form my life was going to take and I held to them—I let the chaos in only when I felt it, only when I needed it in order to feel alive, to appreciate the unexpected, chance, for what it was. I've always been an overly logical person, despite my leanings toward art.

"Let's just be the friends that we are, okay? At least for now anyway," and I reached out my hand to shake on it, to make the whole thing kind of funny, and to reassure Paul that I did like him, 'cause I did. I like him and I always will—I'm strangely, even maniacally, loyal to most of the decisions I make about people, to the way that I feel about them.

So he laughed and said, "Okay," took one of his hands off the steering wheel, and we shook on it. But I don't know if it was ever quite okay for Paul, our only being friends. It's not like he was super unattractive or anything, I mean, he's no knockout, but I've dated other not especially good-looking guys. Paul was pretty nondescript, a doesn't-stand-out-in-a-crowd type of guy. Soft-spoken, chubby, receding hairline, khakis or Dockers, button-down shirts, the full bourgeois jacket—he looked old already at 22—or maybe 23 or 4, or even 25. Come to think of it, I have no idea how old he was. But that's also why I liked hanging out with him. Knowing Paul was like having a smart older brother that I could talk to.

He was one of those professional students, already working on a second degree when I met him. He'd read an incredible number of great books, and so many obscure ones too, that he was a gold mine of information. I learned so much from him and he was always interested in what I was doing too, my performances and everything. Even though we totally disagreed about the state of the art world, I felt that just having the debate, defending our two opposing points of view, and considering the other side, was important to both of us. The more we disagreed and debated the more fun we had, I always thought.

So, maybe because of my vow, or maybe because of who he was, or how he dressed, or who I was then and what I was trying to do, how I wanted to see myself, Paul just wasn't attractive to me in a boyfriend kind of way—like my type or whatever. It never occurred to me to think of him in an intimate context. Paul was my intellectual friend, the one with the briefcase, not really someone you thought of cuddling up with. It even seemed to relax me to be around him, like our meeting of the minds was so sexless that it let me totally forget about my own body and its difference when we were together. Plus I'd already been through a string of intense relationships since getting to college and, frankly, I was emotionally worn out. I felt safe and far away from all that animal boy/girl tension when I was with Paul. It didn't feel like we were in a power struggle either. I always saw our friendship as a meeting of equals.

I especially wasn't going to get intimate with Paul after he confessed to me that he was a virgin. It's hard to believe, I know, but he was pretty shy and only attracted to certain women, or certain types, I guess, so it hadn't ever happened to him. Most of the women he knew must have felt something like the way I did about him—which is a shame, because, let's face it, I think it would have helped

Paul out a lot to get around to losing his virginity. But I wasn't going to be that girl, no way.

It's weird thinking of someone that old still not knowing what sex is like. I can remember that feeling, trying to imagine what it would be like, and then it happening and being nothing at all like you thought it'd be—kind of disappointing actually. But then you get used to it and it is as good as you imagined, only different. Poor Paul, it damaged his credibility somehow, his being a virgin.

Anyway, the night that I was telling you about we were on our way out to Baker Beach. That's where we had most of our intense intellectual dialogues. We'd have dinner somewhere, coffee or dessert after that, and then, around midnight or so, we'd hop into his car, find an open liquor store, grab a bottle of Bordeaux, and cruise on out to the beach. This was our late-night ritual.

On these nights of conversation and debate Paul was like my living encyclopedia. Whatever I wanted to know he could usually tell me, and point me toward the right books to learn more. Let's face it, hanging out with him was much more fun than going to the library: We had food and wine and his big suburban car as transport. He took me to lots of places that this bus rider would never have had the patience to go. I suppose this all sounds pretty self-serving—and it must have been, at least partially—but Paul was so smart, and so kind to me, that I had real affection for him.

You know what? He listened to me and respected my wanting to be an artist and that was rare 'cause I was a 20-year-old, ripped-up leather jacket, snotty little hair-in-the-air chick with a boatload of attitude and artistic pretension. Don't get me wrong: I regret nothing. Still, Paul had always taken me more seriously than most people and that meant a lot to me back then, more than I was actually aware of at the time. I probably acted pretty tough around him too 'cause that's where my head was at: I was in the process of finding out how much harder it is to be respected doing what you want to do when you're a woman and I was taking no prisoners and no shit from anybody.

At one point I remember thinking about telling Paul that I was gay (I was hanging out with Alexis and her crowd a lot back then, and they were all pretty militant, so it might have seemed plausible). But he already knew about Stan, my old boyfriend.

As a matter of fact, that's how I first met Paul, I think. Stan must have introduced us at some point, probably at one of his shows. Then, after he and I had broken up, I'd run into his friends around school. One day I found Paul in the Depot—that's the coffee shop in the student union out at State—and we started talking. We had an hour break at the same time three days a week that semester, so our little chats became a regular thing. Paul usually hung out with this certain group of people in the Depot and eventually we'd join that group during our parallel break 'cause they were his friends and, well, I was interested in meeting a lot of people back then. But the day that we first spoke Paul was sitting there all alone.

Now that I think back on it, he probably wanted to get some homework done that he needed for a class that afternoon. But, well, he never got it done because we talked all during the break and right through our afternoon classes as well. He gave me a lift home afterward, which was pretty far out of his way, and I invited him in for a cup of tea. Alexis and I were going out that night, so we talked some more at my place until she showed up and we all left together, Alexis and I for the movies, and Paul for home back in San Rafael, I guess.

I remember that clique out at school, the one Paul used to hang out with in the Depot. They only accepted me, I'm sure now, because they thought Paul and I were becoming a couple. Then, when we didn't hook up, they started looking at me kind of strangely and finding things wrong with me that they could gossip and talk shit about.

My old boyfriend Stan was never part of that group and even now I don't know how he knew Paul. They certainly weren't anything alike. Stan was a new wave clotheshorse attention-whore, all sharp angles and false intensity, while Paul was a kind of shy, calm, shapeless sort of person. They must have had a class together at some point or something. I knew that we had met before that day in the Depot because Paul knew my name, but I didn't remember his, or anything else about him. I sort of remembered his face, and he seemed innocuous enough, and I guess I didn't feel like sitting alone that day, or maybe all of the tables were occupied, so I said "Hi," or whatever, and sat down with him.

If I remember rightly, we talked about Stan. I was still pretty broken up about that relationship's dissolution, and since Stan was the only thing we knew we had in common, it was a natural starting point. I was venting, no doubt, bitching about how Stan had changed as soon as he'd gotten some notoriety for his act. Seriously, it was a nightmare, like a bad TV movie! The guy suddenly developed this huge ego about his performance thing. Hey, if he was going to be a big one-man-band rock star he had to start acting like a rock star, right? What a joke.

So, I wasn't too thrilled with men in general at the time and that probably helped fuel the way I felt—or didn't feel—about Paul. Sure, I've been on the other end of a crush often enough. But as you get older you learn how to deal with it and not make such a fool of yourself—of course Paul had some catching up to do.

There was this one point, after we'd been friends for a while, when he seemed to be trying to act as if we were a couple in front of other people sometimes, and that was out of line. Maybe he felt like his masculinity was being offended because I hadn't fallen for him, and it was embarrassing for him in front of people who saw us together all the time in the Depot, so he acted like we were more intimate than we actually were. He didn't do it in front of his close friends, or any of my friends, only in front of that crowd in the coffee shop. I guess it was his ego looking out for itself, or maybe he honestly thought that we would start going out at some point and this was a totally natural way to act. Maybe it was one of his warped ways of courting me. As it wasn't threatening or anything, I let it pass—I really didn't care what those people thought.

I've noticed this sort of play-acting with a lot of people; they fucking invent things and then act like their fantasies are real, which is ridiculous. You know, like when people try to tell you what you're thinking or feeling about something. Stan used to do that to me all the time. He'd say things like, "I know you feel threatened," or, "Stop being so paranoid," or some stupid shit like that, like he knew exactly what was going on inside my head if I were upset—and of course it never had anything to do with anything that he'd done. There's nothing worse than being psychoanalyzed by a fucking amateur! And oh, the thing he used to say that really pissed me off was, "I can feel all this hatred that you have for me." What a stupid thing to assume about your partner! He would have liked to believe that my emotions were due to the fact I was out to get him rather than an expression of the hurt and anger I was feeling from all of the fucked-up things he'd done to me. Still, I guess he said it so much I started believing him, or at least acting like I believed him.

It seems to me that most artists don't have this problem as much as other people. It's as if we put our imaginations into something else, our work, and keep it there, outside of our actual lives. Most of my close artist friends are very heavy realists and I like that. They know how to deal with things and how to treat other people. You've got to ask people what's going on with them, not tell them what you think they're feeling or thinking.

Which reminds me of Joyce's daughter, Lucia, or Victor Hugo's, Adele. (It was Paul who told me about them—they were both famously disturbed women.) Carl Jung treated Joyce's daughter, and Joyce even said something like the fantasies that he was working out on paper Lucia seemed to be trying to manifest in real life.

That was exactly the kind of information I got from Paul. He knew a little bit about almost everything. He had one of those fact minds. I couldn't believe the stuff he'd come up with from all of the books he'd read—ancient Greek poets and obscure philosophers I'd never even heard of. I guess all the time the rest of us were out doing drugs and getting laid Paul was at home with a book. Hey, I barely get through the newspaper and the art magazines that keep me up to date with the shows and artists I should know about, and maybe a novel every so often for reading on the bus. I read mostly recent stuff; I have to so I can keep up with what's going on, and I feel like it would be impossible to go back and catch up on all of the classics, unless I get stranded on a desert island or something.

Paul used to joke about hating the twentieth century—like everything was okay until World War I came along and modernism stepped in and it all went to hell. Sometimes I could almost see his point but, well, not really. It does kind of seem like there's a lot more despair and full-scale suffering in the twentieth century than there was before, but I think that we've also broken through so many barriers, artistically and socially. I mean, as a woman, a hundred years ago I probably wouldn't have been able even to go to a university, much less think about art as a career, or have any of the ideas that I have about things. We're moving ahead so much faster now than we were before, that's all, so it's harder for people to adjust to the speed of the changes. Paul was caught up in those old notions that art should always be beautiful and objective, but I love a lot of art that's vicious, ugly, self-centered, and even self-destructive.

"That's the way life goes, Paul," I said to him as he walked around behind the car and headed across the parking lot toward the beach. "It's because you're living now and not then that makes you think things were so much better before. It's like old people who sit around talking about 'the good old days,' forgetting that they were just as miserable then as they are now—it's mostly because they weren't old yet that makes them pine for the past. It's only in retrospect that all that stuff looks so great, not when you're actually living it."

We stepped off the pavement and onto the beach, Paul looking down, kicking at the sand in front of him. "You don't really know what it was like at the turn of the century—you weren't there to see it or feel how the world felt. Everything must have seemed just as fucked-up then as it does now. The rich are always running everything and the middle class being driven into extinction by some Reagan or other. But, hey, here we are! There's always been exploitation, change, and resistance to change. Somehow, we manage to push on through and survive."

"So, I guess I hate life then. Thanks a lot." Every once in a while, Paul adopted a sort of hands-in-the-air attitude, taking what you said as an insult to him personally. It signaled that he was in a bad mood. Sensing that this was going to be one of those nights—a bit of a pity party on his part—I tried to lighten the mood.

"Oh, come on, you know I didn't mean it that way. Although it does seem like you have trouble seeing the positive side of things sometimes. They have cured smallpox, you know."

"Yeah, like conceptual art?" He laughed derisively. "It's just that all this experimentation and stuff that you think is so great is too pretentious for my taste. I have trouble enjoying art that's so contrived and manipulated."

Fighting the urge to pay him back in kind, as this was pretty close to a personal attack, I took a deep breath. "Well," I began, "that's exactly the way I feel when I try to read so many of the so-called 'classics.' They're too conventional, each one imitating the others, no one daring to break the sacred patterns, the hallowed formats, which are mostly only the symptoms of someone's posturing, only it's done in the name of realism or naturalism or whatever." I looked up and down the beach to see if there was anybody sketchy around.

"Can I have some wine?" he asked. I handed him the bottle. While he was drinking, feeling that the evening's debate had pretty much reached an impasse, I got a sudden urge to run off through that loose beach sand, which is so hard to walk in, down to where the foam was sliding up onto the harder packed sand. I wanted to be able to feel and smell the ocean close-up—and not have to struggle with my balance at every step.

I remember that it was one of those super bright nights, a full moon or close to it. I looked to the left at the cliffs of Land's End and the lighthouse, and then across the mouth of the bay toward the Marin headlands and the other lighthouse over there. The Golden

Gate Bridge stretched itself out across the water, way down past the end of Baker Beach, nearly parallel with our path; it looked like a big toy or some kind of matte painting from down here. The wind, too, was making everything feel clean, and the darkness transformed the beach, the ocean, the headlands, and the dotted lights of the houses into a series of backdrops to the stage set that the moon was lighting up on the sand where we strolled. You always forget about the seashell roar of the ocean, too, but you spend your whole time at the beach shouting and hardly realize it until you shut the door and hear the sudden silence inside your car before you drive away.

"Hey!" Paul called out as he trotted down the sand after me.

"It's so beautiful tonight—I can't believe how bright it is."

"But the wind's cold." He kept pulling his pinstriped jacket close around his belly, resting his hands there on his stomach to keep the wind from blowing it open again. He put his collar up too.

"Can I have a sip?" I took a long drink of the sweet white wine and felt fine, warm inside. "Let's walk to the end of the beach, over to the rocks under the bridge."

"Yeah, I'd like to sit down."

"Sit down? On a beautifully brisk night like tonight? Sit down?"

"Well, just for a minute, okay?"

"No, no. You're going to come running with me and work off a little of this." I patted his hands resting on his belly.

"Hey, don't do that."

"I'm sorry. But come on, run with me a little ways."

"You go ahead and I'll catch up."

"Paul."

"I'm sorry, I really don't feel up to it tonight. Can I have some more wine, please?"

"Here. Look, I'm sorry I teased you."

"Don't worry about it—it's okay."

I gave him a look then, a warning. I was getting fed up with his pouting.

"No, really, it's okay," he said and put his arm around me, which wasn't much like him, but a spontaneous gesture I think. It was as if he wanted to reassure me, tell me that it really was okay, what I'd said about his belly. As soon as his arm was lying across my shoulders, though, it was awkward. He didn't know what to do once his arm was resting there and I may have stiffened up, I don't know, because it was such a surprising thing for him to do.

I trusted Paul, you know, but I didn't want to get into a bad situation. I didn't like to be kissed in those days. It felt like men were taking something away from me when they tried to kiss me, as if I had no say in the matter 'cause you're supposed to kiss a boy when you're with him and like it. And it feels pretty awkward to pull away when someone tries to kiss you, to actually physically reject them, so I was trying not to get close enough to anyone for them to try it.

We walked down the beach for what seemed like a long time, talking more small talk, but it didn't feel like anything around us was changing at all, like we were getting anywhere, walking—all of the landmarks were too far away.

"Hey, so tell me about that performance, you know, the thing you did with your friend Alexis that you wouldn't tell me about before." He managed to get his arm down off of my shoulders unobtrusively by stopping to take a drink of wine.

"Oh, that. I don't know if you really want to hear about it, or if I want to talk about it right now."

"Come on, it sounded so intriguing, what I heard you say about it. What could be so weird?"

"It's pretty weird. I mean, most people think it's kind of disgusting."

"I know you pretty well. I'm not going to freak out or anything."

"OK—but you asked for it." I took a deep breath and started to tell him about it: "Do you remember when I told you I wanted to do a performance piece that reflected the things that I thought were the real parts of what I've learned so far about life and art, and the people who taught me more abstract, ineffable things, as opposed to my formal university education?"

"Yeah."

"Well, I decided that I wanted to combine two things into a ritualistic performance. First, I had the idea to make some sort of tribute to the people who have taught me special things. I also wanted to learn some new skill that I'd need in order to perform the piece, to back up the concept that the performance would be about learning skills and putting practical knowledge to use. I wanted that knowledge to be something I would actively seek out and learn for myself from someone I chose to teach me, instead of being passively taught things that other people think are important for me to know, like the way we're taught in school.

"Then I was reading something for my mythology class about the ancient mystery religions, and it mentioned that cult members worshiping the earth goddess Cybele used to drink each other's blood as a sort of tribute to the goddess. That seemed to me like a kind of beautiful gesture—and, well, challenging too. I'm pretty squeamish by nature, and I thought it would be interesting if I could learn to overcome my squeamishness as part of the performance, a kind of self-teaching through familiarity and repetition, you know, trial and error.

"Everything fell into place then. I drafted a script in which I learn how to draw blood, using all the modern medical techniques, and then I use that skill to take some blood from people who I admire, which I then drink in a ritual of sharing and tribute—and if the whole experience helped me to get over my squeamishness and fear of blood, then I wouldn't only have to learn a skill to be able to do the performance, but I'd be learning in a sense, too, *while* I was doing the piece, and that was perfect."

I waited, but Paul didn't say anything. When he finally looked up from the ground, "Wow" was what he said, smiling at me kind of crookedly, like he was impressed but also skeptical.

"So," I went on, "this friend of mine who's a nurse taught me how to draw blood and I set the whole thing up, using my friend Alexis, as my first, I don't know, partner, I guess. I got my roommate to photo-document the whole thing. I wanted to do it privately the first time, and then actually to perform the subsequent partners as public rituals, varying the settings each time to suit the people to whom I wanted to pay tribute. It seemed better to start this way both as a trial run and also because Alexis and I have a pretty private relationship, and she had to be the first 'cause we're so close—and of course it had a lot to do with trust."

"And you did it?"

"Well, sort of. I mean, yeah, I drew her blood and we put it into this beautiful crystal chalice and I took a couple of sips and then this terrible feeling that I'd made some sort of a mistake descended on the room."

"Really?"

"Yeah, it didn't feel right at all—it was weird. Plus blood congeals a lot faster than you'd think and the glass got all thick and cloudy and I couldn't finish drinking it and that kind of spoiled the performance.

"Poor Alexis was sitting there with a lump of her blood in a chalice and in these little vials and like doom all around, and I felt kind of bad about the whole thing. I didn't expect that to happen at all. We didn't know what to do. It was pretty weird."

"That's so interesting."

"It taught me something—not what I expected to learn—but something."

"Like what?"

"I can't explain it exactly, but it's like a mistake that I won't make again."

"How did Alexis take it?"

"Pretty well. She mostly shrugged it off, but I was afraid for a while how it was going to affect our friendship. I do feel like I owe her something now. I mean, I'd be a lot quicker to do something she asked me to do than I would have been before."

Paul laughed at that and I kind of smiled back, I guess, but I didn't think it was all that funny. I was still worried then that Alexis was mad at me about how the tribute performance had gone but we hadn't spoken of it directly. I certainly wasn't going to bring it up if I didn't have to. I was waiting on her, to see if it was a real problem that we would have to deal with or just something we'd forget about after a while. I should have known better, and I guess we never did get it straight. It's still sort of a problem between us, maybe only the fact that we've never discussed it.

We had almost come to the rocks way down at the end of the beach, right up under the Golden Gate. We stood looking at the brightly lit bridge looming overhead for a while and Paul said, "I still don't know about performance art. When you explain everything behind one of your pieces it's perfectly clear and fascinating and all that, but when I see someone doing one it usually comes off as pointless to me—without an explanation it's impossible to figure out what it's all about."

"Do you always have to understand things? I don't think you have to understand a person's reason for doing a performance to enjoy the piece while it's happening, to appreciate it."

"I think that I naturally want to follow a work of art though, to get more out of it by thinking about what it's about as well as experiencing it. A painter chooses the subject of his painting, right? And that subject is as important as the colors he uses, or the style he paints in. With performance art I don't know what the real subject is most of the time so I just see a pointless exercise in form."

"Not if it's an abstract painting. Even in most still lifes the subject is often pretty much arbitrary. And what about music? Lots of people enjoy music who have no idea how it's constructed, how scales and chords work, how it's all mathematically based."

"Yeah, I guess that's true. I wish I was better at the piano."

He was probably thinking about the opera that he wanted to write. I still can hardly believe that Paul actually wanted to write an opera. No one else I've ever met from our generation even likes listening to opera, much less wants to write one. Sometimes we'd drive around in his car listening to Wagner's *Ring* series. He wanted to write a novel too; it was going to be set at the turn of the century and go up to the First World War, when Paul thought everything went all to hell in the Western world, a kind of "end of the world as we know it" tale.

"Oh, come on, cheer up," I said. "Take the bottle, have some more wine."

"Thanks."

We were at the rocks now and it occurred to me again that we shouldn't just be standing around on such a beautiful and exuberant night, that we were wasting the unnaturally bright moonlight.

"Come on—let's go swimming."

It had suddenly struck me. I wanted to do something crazy and exciting, something stupid maybe, and to do it all the way. "Come on, Paul, it'll do you good." Maybe I was only joking at first, but the more Paul tried to shrug me off, the more serious I got.

"You're kidding, I hope."

I guess I don't take being treated like a child very well. As if adulthood were only an excuse for not doing anything interesting anymore, or anything at all. "No, I'm not. Come on! For once in your life take a chance and do something crazy."

"Do you have any idea how cold it is in that water, how dangerous it is to swim here, even in the daytime—much less at night?"

I started taking off my clothes. No, it didn't register with me at the time that I probably shouldn't have been stripping in front of Paul. I was doing it totally spontaneously—I really wanted to go swimming. It's the not thinking about being naked that gets you to forget about being embarrassed. In a performance or when you do art modeling you have to concentrate on what you're doing and forget about being naked. I'd pretty much gotten over it.

Paul kept trying to talk me out of going into the water, once he saw I was seriously stripping down to go swimming, but I wanted to show him something about living, about being in the moment and taking chances, so I laid my clothes out on the rocks and ran down the beach a ways to where it was smooth and I went down quickly into the water. Paul came up to where the surf was finishing on the sand and rolling back into the sea and he yelled at me not to go all the way in. But I dove under when I got to where it was deep enough. I never went out any further than where the water was up to my chest, but I crouched down to get my whole body under so it would all be the same temperature and I wouldn't feel the wind as much. Yeah, it was cold, fucking freezing! I was totally numb in seconds. But it felt good too, each wave coming in at me, sliding up against my body, pushing me back toward the beach, the big ones going right over my head. It was great, that feeling of power so strong and regular, the moon brighter in the sky now that I was out in the middle of the dark water.

"Ah, the fucking universe! Woooooo!" I screamed, adrenaline coursing through every limb.

Paul was still standing at the edge of the beach yelling something at me that I couldn't hear over the waves, looking worried. Of course, in retrospect, I know it was a stupid thing to do, but I wanted to see him come in, so I put my head underwater and started splashing around like I was in trouble. I made a pretty good show of it, too—I didn't yell "Help!" or anything like that, which would have made it totally unbelievable—and I knew Paul was watching me, worrying about me. I gasped for air, like I couldn't call out, and pretended to be pulled under by a wave.

Then, when I looked up and saw him taking off his coat and dropping his shoes frantically in the sand like Clark Kent changing into Superman, I thought that I was being stupid. I didn't want Paul to play the hero, Popeye to my Olive Oyl, I wanted him to learn to be crazy and to appreciate the rush you can get out of life if you let yourself go once in a while. Poor Paul, I could see that he was seriously worried that I might be in trouble, and I didn't even know if he could swim. It occurred to me, too, that I was taking advantage of the fact that he cared about me and I didn't want to do that either. He looked so awkward trying to get his pants off, with his chubby belly and all. So I got out of the water and ran up to stop him.

"I'm okay, I'm okay. I was only kidding. I was just trying to get you to come in and swim with me."

"Oh," and he looked at me. He was so forlorn—his shirt half unbuttoned and his pants around his feet—that I had to hug him. I felt bad. I wanted to make it all right. But then I felt his face and his breath against my neck, and I was naked and everything. I guess I kind of pushed him away, stepped back, and ran over to the rocks to get my clothes.

When I'd finished putting my clothes back on, I looked over and Paul was sitting there on the sand, the water washing up around his legs, his head bent down. He was moving the sand around in the water with his hand, playing with it. Oh, what have you done, Kate, I thought, what have you done.

10/1985
San Francisco

7: THE IDEA

Would they let me run, though, if I wanted to run? What about some room in which to move, a city full of empty spaces into which we can all dig our own little burrows? Or a way of life into which we could poke some holes? A single great contradiction, maybe. An idea.

Do they care too much or not at all? Could I fly like in Chagall? My father used to scream because, as a child, I went around breaking the windows in every room of the house.

I put my father's name beside my mother's and one is longer. In this crowd I grow two more faces – I'm surrounded. I neglect everything for the woman; I neglect the woman for all of the other things there are to love.

You may have noticed that everyone's gone now. That happens – it doesn't have to be a tragedy. Left alone the pieces will let go of one another and move off in different directions. Each adept takes their piece of the broken jug, their tesserae, for future recognition. I could always try to pull the pieces back together. I might even be able to rest in-between efforts, if it's not too late. If that doesn't work, I may only have to try again. It could always be as simple as that.

DEVIN WANTS TO MAKE A MOVIE

I. SNATCHES OF DIALOGUE

Devin

I guess we'll have to do it on videotape.

* * *

Johnny

You can't do good work when you're on speed—you're like this all the time. You rush through everything and it all comes out sloppy and...

* * *

Devin

I broke Emma's door down because she wouldn't answer it—she was asleep. I was totally flipped out, I guess. After I left her house I went out onto Fell Street, jumped onto the hood of this lady's car, swung my sword over my head and demanded a ride Downtown. Emma was pretty nice about the whole thing, though. She told me, "Devin, you just don't *do* things like that. Come back later, when I ask you to."

Johnny

You were carrying a sword?

* * *

Devin

It's like a new lease on life. I'm trying to say, "Hey, it's okay—you're all right. All you have to do is get along and try to be happy." It's also a kind of working through.

* * *

Johnny

I'm worried about Devin.

* * *

Devin

And Emma broke up with me while I was in jail that first time. That didn't help any.

* * *

Devin

Yeah, my landlord came in early one morning—I was asleep—and there were syringes and drugs spread out all over the place, on the floor, everywhere. I said, "Relax, you'll get the rent, just get the fuck out of here! Fucking get out!"

* * *

Johnny

When he's OK he's a total sweetheart, but there's something kinda sad, I don't know, tragic about the guy.

* * *

Devin

I ran because I was afraid. The first time they arrested me the police beat the crap out of me. When I got to the edge of the roof and they were coming up behind me...

* * *

Devin

Yeah, I'm out. My court date's in two weeks. I think it'll be okay. It's my first offense and all—and I only walked out of the place with a Chinese-American dictionary.

* * *

Marguerite

Devin is driving me crazy with all these phone calls. He wants to start some kind of band when he gets out of the hospital, but I don't quite understand.

* * *

Johnny

Yeah, Keira rejecting him had a lot to do with that first time he started blowing it and getting all psychotic on us. That was more than a year ago, probably almost two years now. She never knew that it affected him that much though.

* * *

Devin

No, I really shouldn't talk about it until after my court date.

* * *

Devin

I want to use the work of all of my friends—everyone I know on the art scene—in the movie. I want it to be a huge project pulling together all kinds of similar but unique ideas and disciplines. I'd love to have everyone working directly on it, but some people are going to do outside things and I'll incorporate them into the whole later. Adrian is going to do the music, and there's a song of Johnny's that I'd like to use, maybe get his band to perform for the film.

* * *

Eric

I heard that some wino bit off one of Devin's fingernails while he was in detox. That's disgusting. I don't know how he gets himself into these things.

* * *

Devin

I've been working on this series of paintings, pastels actually.

* * *

Keira

That fucked-up creep—I hope I never hear from him again. Good riddance. What a self-absorbed asshole. Hey, let's destroy ourselves and then ask other people to pick up the pieces—as if we owed it to him because he was such a devoted and good friend to us all the time we've known him. Fuck that! He expects me to be all blown away and comforting about the mess he's in when it's all totally his own fucking fault. I said, "Hey, man, I don't owe you anything and I think you're a stupid fuck for what you've done." And he said, "Hey, I paid a dime to call you, that's something right there!" Can you believe that guy?

* * *

Devin

I wish Lee could forgive Adrian and all so that they could work together again. I'd like to get Lee more in on the film.

* * *

Johnny

You gotta pity the guy.

* * *

Devin

I went into a market, grabbed a bottle of wine, said, "I'm taking this and there's nothing you can do about it," and ran out. I don't know how I made it all the way back Downtown.

* * *

Devin

It needs some highlighting, and a little work on the reclining figure. Yeah, it does need some work, I think, but I can do it anytime. I'd like to enter it in this drawing contest that the *Bay Guardian* is having soon. It'll only take a second to fix it up, and then it'll be really good.

* * *

Johnny

What am I, the guy's father? I don't know how to help him.

Maggie

What did he do?

Johnny

Broke into a pharmacy.

* * *

Devin

Basically, there are two kinds of people on the San Francisco art scene—and I want to show them both in the movie, but kinda from my perspective, or the perspective of the protagonist—sort of my persona. As I see it, there are the speed people and the Europe people. The Europe people work in these prestigious jobs that don't pay very much, like bookstores and art galleries, until they get enough money together to go to Paris, London, Berlin, or wherever, to become great artists. They go, most of them—well, some of them never even make it, and I guess some of them *do* do something—but most of them seem to come back eventually and I don't think they really gain anything over there. A lot of them come back feeling like they somehow failed in Europe.

The speed people are more into making money: They need these high-paying jobs to keep themselves in drugs all the time. They're like waitresses and construction workers, stuff like that. They're not "cool" at all on their jobs, but they're always doing some kind of art on the side and going to all of the openings and to the right nightclubs and stuff. They're always moving in circles, you know, around and around and around.

* * *

Johnny

Devin's in jail again.

* * *

Devin

That one's my letter to my friends. See, it's in letter format. A sort of "Hi, everybody, I'm back and I'm okay."

* * *

Johnny

How'd you get those scars?

Devin

That's from when the construction workers beat me up.

Johnny

What for? What did you do?

Devin

I don't want to talk about it. I got beat up like three times that day—I was tweaked out.

* * *

Johnny

I tried to tell him, "Hey, just because you broke your leg in seven places running from the police and are stretched out on a hospital bed for God knows how long doesn't mean people have to suddenly like you."

* * *

Devin

Yeah, we had a lot of problems getting together. But Keira is sweet—I love her, I do! At first she didn't want to sleep with me, then she did, and then, when we finally did, she felt all weird about it afterward. When we did it she was crying and upset, but I didn't force her or anything.

* * *

Devin

It's getting better all the time. The drugs are slowly draining out of my blood and into bedpans. I'm beginning to calm down enough, get straight enough, to be able to read again. I watch a lot of TV and talk on the phone.

* * *

Johnny

"I came, I saw, I took a nap." What's that?

Devin

That's going to be in the movie. It's what my friend Joel wrote to me from Europe when he finally got there. He never left the hotel room.

* * *

Peter

I'm Peter Connell, Devin Connell's father. I'm trying to locate my son. Would you have any idea where he's staying?

Johnny

I think he's living with our friend Eric. I have his number here somewhere.

Peter

No, that's who I just now spoke with, and he told me that Devin isn't staying with him anymore and that you might know where he is.

Johnny

No sir, the last I heard of him he was at Eric's.

* * *

Devin

It's just as well that she's left. I mean, Emma is only fifteen, so every time we made love it was statutory rape—and I really need that, you know, considering my position.

II. A SETTING

A white-on-white corridor inside San Francisco General Hospital, six or eight doors set close together along its length. At the hallway's dead end, where it separates into a T-shape, there are two semi-private rooms going off in separate directions. Devin is in the right-hand room. The other bed in his room, the one nearest the door, is vacant; its light blue sheets are stretched tight across its foam mattress, the bed-back bent slightly, as if to support someone in a half-sitting position—maybe to watch the enormous television hung from the wall at an angle in the opposite corner. A former patient has kindly donated the TV set to the room.

There's a table on wheels to the left of Devin's bed and a long empty space between his bed, the table, and the door. The room is quite large actually, but the beds being set away from the walls, the low ceiling, the bulky movable tables, and the fact that there's only the one narrow row of windows, give it a cramped, but not a cluttered feel. Like most workplaces, it's functional and impersonal.

The television is on, its changing colors flashing across the half-closed curtains meant to form an imaginary wall between Devin's half of the room and the other, vacant half. The pleats in the partition are dark—the lone row of windows in the room are next to Devin's bed, but the sun is busy setting in the West, on the other side of the hospital. The open, empty space around Devin's bed is filled with a flat, drab, reflected light. The bulging edges of the curtains change from blue to red to yellow as the images on the TV screen dart from scene to scene.

Devin lolls uncomfortably in his bed in a propped-up position. He can look out the windows to his right by raising his head a little. The table on his left, just a bit higher than the bedclothes, is close by should he need anything from it. Directly in front of the foot of his bed looms the television, easily manipulated by the remote control lying on the table with all of the rest of his things.

Four enormous sheets of art paper are tacked to the long white wall to the television's left, directly in front of Devin's bed, a pastel drawing on each of them. Devin claims that the works are "a representation of the interlocking themes of the process of my recovery."

The first piece in the series, in soft shades of red, pink, and light blue, vaguely, expressionistically depicts the face of a woman, a tear dangling from the bottom lid of her left eye. There's writing all around the central image. The words begin in the upper-left-hand corner with "Dear...," and end in the bottom-right-hand corner with Devin's signature.

Another of the pastel drawings represents the view one would have from the television's perch high up in the corner of the room. The figure in the bed is obviously meant to represent Devin himself, although the section of the figure's chest that's visible beneath the pajamas isn't flesh, but rather bone—the sternum and rib cage—and a dark, grinning death's head sits atop its shoulders. The figure's hands are flesh, but inert, their long fingers at rest on either side of the thighs. This picture, the artist explains, was drawn the day his ex-girlfriend Emma, who had broken up with him and left town while he was in jail, returned to San Francisco with her new boyfriend.

There's another drawing taped onto the center pane of the windows, next to the bed. This is an older picture, one of the few things a friend has been able to salvage from Devin's abandoned apartment. It's a portrait of Emma, painted in dark colors, a mass of permed brown hair drooping past one of her eyes and casting a shadow over her cheek to the ridge of her nose. The figure's other eye shines out brightly, as does her smile; the girl's head is apparently resting on her palm, but it's not tilted in that direction, so the effect is more like someone touching their own cheek to see how it feels, or to enjoy how it feels.

By now the sun has finished setting and the unoccupied portion of the room has gone totally black, except when it's lit up by a particularly bright scene flashing across the TV. You can still see the last grayish light of the day brushing the architectural details of the Victorian flats in rows outside, through the windows, across the freeway on the inland side of Potrero Hill.

Devin has switched on the lamp that comes out of the wall above his bed. On the table below, now brightly illuminated, are several empty cans of an orange soft drink, one half-empty can, two empty packs of cigarettes, a disposable lighter, a Dixie cup, and several spare pain pills for emergencies. There's also a green push-button telephone and an open box of pastels, some of the crayons scattered over the Formica table surface and others nestled in the folds of Devin's blanket.

The blanket covering Devin's left leg and abdomen is thin and slipping off of the bed because he's constantly squirming around to get at the phone, his cigarettes, the pastel crayons, or his orange drink. At any rate, he only needs the blanket on his left side from the waist down, as his right leg is covered by an enormous plaster cast. The cast is decorated with drawings and comments made mostly with the pastel crayons by his friends and the many acquaintances who've come by the hospital to visit. The leg is in traction, hung from a pole running above the bed by a nylon cord that goes through a pulley system, balanced by plastic bags filled with water dangling at the foot of the bed. The nylon cords are anchored to a steel pin that passes through Devin's cast, as well as his ankle. The bones of the leg in suspension, he tells us, are broken in seven separate places.

Devin has hooked his art pad to the pole running above his bed so that it's always within reach—otherwise it would completely cover the bedside table. He's taken the pad down now, curled his left, free leg up, and propped the pad against his raised knee. He draws, picking up and discarding the crayons scattered about the bedclothes, as he needs them. The picture that he's working on will be the fifth and final part of the series hanging on the wall. This drawing will be about escaping, according to the artist. It will depict two figures—probably a man and a woman, a couple maybe, but it'll be hard to tell exactly because of the darkness of the nighttime scene—one standing guard while the other sleeps, a burning city in the background. Devin will never get around to actually finishing this segment of his series of drawings.

His hands move in short sure strokes across the paper, but his mind is somewhere else. It's running through memories and reflecting, going over things he's done—or thinks he's done, or doesn't remember having done but people have told him that he's done. He's retracing each step along the path that's lead him to this hospital bed. These memories make him wonder about what will happen next, to make plans, to dream. He's trying to decide who his real friends are, what he can learn from them, how they can all contribute to the movie that he wants to make about the San Francisco art scene. Then his mind goes back again, revisiting the events that snowballed into his breakdown and his now patient process of recovery. He wonders about old friends he's not sure of anymore, or hasn't seen in years, and these thoughts eventually bring him forward in time, up to his present state, and he again acknowledges the television, the empty bed on the other side of the room, the picture he's drawing on the pad leaning up against his knee, and the lit-up windows of the Victorian homes of Potrero Hill out the window. Then, running off again, his thoughts will come back up against the inevitable wall of the future in front of him, the terribly slow process of healing, and the ever-closer terminus of his approaching court date.

III. JOHNNY'S VOICE-OVER NARRATION

Scene One

I hung out with Devin mostly in that in-between time, right after Mary had gone back to Scotland and before I met and moved in with Maggie. I even crashed at 86 Golden Gate for a while, starting the night of Mary's going-away party when everything got all fucked up between my roommates Severus and Pantha and me. We spent Mary's last couple of weeks in San Francisco in Devin and Adrian's space at 86 and I just stayed on, like a zombie, for a few months after she'd gone. I was still in the Air Force then and technically living up on the base in Fairfield for most of the week. So, when things finally got a little strained in that tiny cluttered room with the shaky lofts, I moved my stuff into my old room at my mom's apartment in the projects in Chinatown and stayed there on the weekends until I got out of the service and Maggie and I found a place together Downtown.

I guess Devin had already started tweaking out by then. I mean, the guy goes overboard with everything. He binges on speed—he'd started shooting it again, so it's no wonder he freaks out. But, what the hell, am I his father? I don't know how to help the guy. I'd like to, but people almost always do what they want to do, or what they think they need to do. It's pretty much impossible to affect someone—and if you do it's usually by accident. Hey, everybody makes their own life, you know, we all make our own decisions and we have to look out for ourselves. That's my philosophy anyway.

It didn't seem like there was anything especially wrong with Devin that night, like he was on the edge of freaking out or anything, but the more I think about it now, the more signs I can see in the way he was acting that he was gearing up for something.

He had found a way to get into the old pool hall all on his own. It's right across the street from 86, in that wedge of buildings where Market Street meets Golden Gate at that weird angle. There's a parking lot closing up the triangle on the Jones Street side, and we were walking through it on our way back to 86 after dinner at Tu-Lan's. I was feeling totally bloated and relaxed from eating a big meal of their great Vietnamese food—you know, like when you wanna stretch out and go to sleep it feels so good. We'd been ravenous and had eaten too much too fast and were talking about trying to walk it off by going to a bar somewhere when Devin looks up at the billboard above the parking lot. It's all lit up, a stupid light-house by the sea advertising a fucking bank or something, looming there above the dark and quiet parking lot, and he says, "Hey, Johnny, you wanna shoot a few games of pool?" Which sounds good 'cause I'm expecting the thick Vietnamese coffee that we've just had to kick in any minute and make us all energetic and shit, and I think he's talkin' about heading over to the Savoy Tivoli in North Beach, or maybe walking over to that place on Polk, the gay bar with the two cheap pool tables in the back. Instead, he points at the billboard and the building behind it and says, "I finally found a way to get in."

'Cause we used to sit around at 86 all the time, when Adrian was still living there, getting drunk and hanging out and we'd look out the window and see the old dark neon sign on top of the building across the street advertising "COCHRAN'S POOL AND BILLIARD HALL." That sign hadn't been lit-up in God knows how long, and the door to the place was chained up and had become a urinal of sorts, for those too lazy to get to the parking lot and piss more privately behind the cars. And we always threatened to go over there and try to find a way to get in, to see if there was anything left of it. The subject usually came up around the time we were getting bored lying around drinking, but always after we were too drunk or worn out from playing music to actually do anything about it.

"You did?" I said, following Devin's pointing finger to the lighthouse shining its amber searchlight across the stormy sea of mutual funds up above our heads. Man, that billboard was huge and put out a lot of light—I don't know how anybody had the nerve to go into the porn theater across the street.

"Yeah, I found a way into that pool hall up on the second floor," Devin tells me, "and it's perfect. They never moved the tables or cues or any of that stuff out. It's totally cool. We can play all night if we want to."

"How do we get in? Is it hard?"

Devin led me over to one of the girders holding the billboard up against the back wall of the triangular building. "I made a sort of ladder by sawing a saw-tooth pattern into this long flat board I found. You lean it here into the corner of the I-beam and walk up it like stairs, using your hands on the beam for balance, like this, to pull yourself up until you're high enough to grab the ladder." I could see the ladder hanging out from under the billboard's catwalk about fifteen or twenty feet up, like a fire escape ladder. "Then you just climb up to the catwalk and walk across it, around the billboard, and jump over onto the roof. Easy as that."

"How do you get in from the roof?"

"Come on." He started pulling me on toward 86 again and explaining, more excitedly now. "There's a, I guess, fire escape kind of thing in the bathroom—it's got like a hatch. You open it and slide down the pipes against the wall like going down a rope. Here," he handed me two bills, "you go get us some beer and I'll go up to my place and get the board."

He ran across the street then and went into the elaborate 86 door-unlocking procedure—and since there's no buzzer or anything like that, I yelled over to him to leave it open. He nodded before charging on into the purple doorway and up that long single flight of stairs where I'd followed him like a million times. I could see that endless narrow passage of green shag carpeting that had such a long way to go to clear the height of the movie theater at ground level. I had heard that the big open space, where all of the lofts are now, used to be a gym. Well, half the workout woulda been trippin' up those stairs just to get to it.

I went around the corner to one of the liquor stores on Turk and got a forty of the Green Death and a sixer of Elephant, and then went back out into the night. It was all flashing lights on Turk Street, idiots standing around getting drunk, coming up to ya, gotta talk to ya, trying to get something offa ya, cars rushing by, ogling the ladies. Somebody somewhere had a radio blasting mostly static. I felt pretty good, kinda adventurous and ready to climb. What the hell, if Devin had gotten into and out of this place before and it'd been okay, well, then, it was probably all right. And what's trespassing? The worst it could be was a night in jail and it probably wouldn't even be that. So what the hell, I'm thinking, let's do it. I guess the beers I'd had with dinner and that Vietnamese coffee were swirling around together inside me by now 'cause I felt like a rush and kinda fucked up at the same time. I lit a cigarette to keep the buzz on and walked back around the corner to 86.

By the time I got there the door was locked. I was about to go across the street to the payphone in the parking lot to call Devin and make him come down and let me in—which I hate to do, you know, 'cause it's so disgusting in that parking lot and I think guys piss on the phone for fun—when I remember that I still have my old keys from when I was living there.

The next thing I know I'm climbing up those old familiar stairs for the first time in months and the smell of the place is coming back to me, right up from the rotting carpet left over from the fucking '70s. It doesn't smell like any other place I've ever been in; it's not like bars or clubs, you know, beer and leather and dampness and all of 'em the same. 86 is a sort of unique collection of odors: the dusty old shag carpet like somebody's parents' house in the suburbs, plus a little of that beer and leather from the punks, and all the paint and turpentine from the artists' apartments, and the sheet rock and stolen lumber that everything in there is built out of, surrounded on its edges by the lingering smell of the sweaty gym that the space used to be.

There was a lot of junk stacked on the landing (as usual), building supplies and furniture that people were throwing out. As I went by the doors down the crooked makeshift hallway I remembered what the inside of each space was like and the people who'd lived in them when I'd been staying there. Down at the end of the hallway was

Devin's room, the cheapest and smallest of them all; I could hear him moving stuff around behind the thin sheet rock walls. Devin's space was kinda like a tree fort that a bunch of kids had built in a grammar school gymnasium and it had always been the worst in the building: the most cramped, the messiest, and the one with the shabbiest lofts and the most dangerous wiring. Still, I'd never seen it like this. "Jesus," I said laughing, "what happened here?"

"What?" Devin looked up, almost like he didn't quite understand what I was talking about. "Oh, this? Yeah, well, I had it completely clean, and then there were a couple of great dumpsters in the neighborhood, you know."

"What the hell are you going to do with all this shit?"

"A lot of it, like the concrete and wood, is construction and art material. I want to get rid of these stupid loft beds Adrian and I built in such a hurry when we first moved in and make a really good loft. And this window is so big I want to put a balcony outside of it."

"That sounds cool. Do you know how to build it so it won't fall down?"

"Sure. What kind of beer did you get?"

"The beer of your homeland" (Devin had grown up in Seattle) "and a six pack of Elephant."

"Rainier? Jesus, we could do better than that!"

"Mostly it was for old times' sake. You got an opener?"

"Somewhere."

Devin had already found his saw-toothed board, which, because it was pretty big and the room so small, hadn't taken much of an effort. But the can opener took forever to find, and then we decided we needed a backpack to carry the beer in, and we had to have some music. So we opened two of the beers and started searching through the wreckage that covered the floor for a backpack, a tape deck, and some tapes to play.

"I like your, eh, friend here." He had a female-shaped mannequin lying on its back on some cinder blocks in the center of the room.

"Yeah, thanks. Right now she's Sally the fallen angel prostitute. She was Sally the angel—I had her strung up to the ceiling, but she fell down and her wings got crushed and they were too fucked-up to fix."

"Here's the backpack—hand me the beers," I said, trying to get all of our shit together. Devin threw his saw-toothed board over his shoulder and we went down, out, across the street and back through the parking lot to the base of the billboard. Amazingly, Devin's plan worked perfectly. We leaned the board in the inside corner of the I-beam, its saw-tooth pattern giving us footholds, and grabbed onto the backside of the beam with our hands to pull ourselves up. Devin ran right up the edge of the board like it was a stairway, hardly using his hands at all. He was going too fast and had to jump up to the hanging ladder above in one quick lunge as the board kicked out from under him. Still, his hands caught the bottom rung; he did this amazingly athletic chin-up, curled his leg around the rung, and made it onto the ladder like some sort of enormous noisy insect going up a wall.

"Hey, slow down, dude"—I was trying to get the board back into place. "Here, take the backpack so I can get up." I tossed it up to him and he went off again, straight up the ladder like a shot.

I climbed the I-beam on the stair-step board too and when I got to the ladder I yelled, "Hey, Devin, do I leave the board down there?"

"Yeah," he hollered back, never turning around, "just leave it."

It was a long way up that rickety ladder and it didn't feel very secure with Devin bouncing along like a maniac above me—then someone yelled at us from the parking lot. You know, "Get down from up there!" or some parental crap like that. I shrugged up at Devin when he looked back. "It's only one of those chicken-shit valet parking dudes; he's only kidding." I wasn't so sure, but we kept on climbing just the same.

When we got up to the scaffolding at the foot of the billboard it was okay to look down 'cause there was at least a little something under our feet now, and a railing. We hopped over to the flat, tar-paper roof of the building and walked around the edges for a while, checking out the view of Market Street, which we only ever saw from the sidewalk.

"This reminds me of when I was in high school," I told him. "We used to sit around on the roof of that old grammar school over at Hyde and Sutter and drink tequila."

"Come on, the hatch's over here somewhere." Devin takes me over to this wooden box-thing that we lift up together, like a hatbox lid, and you could see about a foot-and-a-half space between the roof and the drop ceiling and then a black nothingness below that. We got some newspapers from somewhere, lit them on fire with my lighter, and dropped 'em into the hole so that we could see how far down the floor was, and Devin went right in. I dropped the lighter down to him quickly, before the newspaper had time to burn itself out, and he used that to get over to the circuit board and he lit the whole place up. The blank space below turned into a bathroom, as Devin had promised, and I slid down a pole to the top of a urinal and hopped onto the floor.

Cochran's Pool Hall was huge inside: all the tables, cues, the scoring pegs, barstools, nearly everything, intact. Even the Coke and pinball machines and a snack bar with a fryer for French fries and an old '50s milkshake blender were sitting on the counter untouched. They looked like they were just waiting for the short-order cook to come in and fire 'em up. I couldn't believe that the place had never been cleaned out or ransacked. It was right outta *The Hustler* or something. And, oh, the funniest thing was that the little book the place had used to write out their payroll checks was sitting open by the cash register; it was as if the last thing they had done before closing up forever was to pay everybody off. The checks were personalized "COCHRAN'S POOL AND BILLIARD HALL," with their motto underneath, "Home of the Hustlers."

Before anything else, Devin took out the tape recorder—he knew right where to plug it in—put on Killing Joke's first album, and I opened up two beers. The only thing missing were balls. For some reason there weren't that many of them, and the few that were left were in two different sizes. I guess a ball is the easiest pool hall item to take away with you—and there was some garbage lying around as if someone had been in there before us, even a spot where it looked like they had tried to build a fire to keep warm maybe. I didn't ask Devin if it'd been him.

He got real pissed about the balls being two different sizes and threw one across the room. It was funny; the walls were so heavily wallpapered—or so cheap—that the ball made this thick thud, went about a half an inch into the plaster, sat there for a second, and then dropped gently onto the floor. Pretty anticlimactic.

"Mellow out, Devin. So we'll have two sizes of balls, no big deal."

There was still a rack in every table, as far as I could see, and everything in its place. Some of the panels of the drop ceiling had fallen in here and there so we had to hunt around for the cleanest-looking table. "Man, these Olympic-size tables are too fucking big," I told Devin.

"Maybe."

"Maybe?" I said. "You been practicing or what? You don't sink anything by accident on these bastards, and you can hardly see from one end to the other for the cigarette smoke."

"All right, how 'bout this one?"

"Yeah, looks okay." I ran my hand across the felt and it seemed pretty smooth, but even the smaller tables looked extra big, I guess because I'm so used to playing in bars, and this whole place was so enormous—with the high ceiling and all—and because there was only me and Devin and twenty or so empty tables in it.

Usually, when I'm not up on the base, I play at the Savoy Tivoli, where they have two tiny tables and it's always crowded—unless you go in the early afternoon. Or that place we found on Polk Street, the old Western-style gay bar called the Roundup, which has two tables in a back room that's been totally forgotten by the older regulars who hang out up at the bar. It still only costs a quarter there and they make these incredibly cheap Long Island Ice Teas in canning jars. One's enough for a whole evening of fun.

I brushed the table clean while Devin hunted around for some chalk and picked out a couple of not-too-warped cues.

It was quiet for a couple of minutes and I was thinking about one afternoon when I had gone to the Savoy with Kate and showed her the basics of how to shoot pool. She picked it up pretty quickly and the more we drank the better we got. We were both bummed that afternoon, she about breaking up with Stan and me all fucked-up over Mary having to go back to Scotland, and Annette was doing too much speed and driving me crazy with all of her invented problems, and it felt good just to hang out with someone, shoot some pool, drink, and talk. It had been such a beautiful afternoon too, as I remembered it. There's this perfect half an hour or so at the Savoy, right after they open up, when the sun comes down under the awning of the patio but hasn't quite gone below the roofs of the flats across the street, when the place lights up with long shadows and that great feeling of the end of the day. It makes you want to stretch out and let go and wait 'til the night comes in and you can start all over again.

"You break 'em up, dude," I said while Devin was racking up the balls. He did, but he took the shot in a rush and hit the cue ball too hard and caught the rack too far to one side, only one or two balls splitting out at the corners. That pissed him off and he broke his cue over the edge of the table next to ours.

"Hey, Devin, calm down—you're scaring me."

"Don't worry about it, we've got plenty of cues." He spread his arms out and behind him there was a long rack, like a whole wall of cues, a couple of hundred of them hung up in a row like a picket fence.

"All right, but just don't break 'em all, okay?"

How could I get mad at the guy? He was only playing around, and he had that cute little boy grin and everything. So I took my shot and said, "OK, I'm solids."

"I guess that means I'm stripes," he said, circling the table, looking for a shot.

I shot twice more and said, "Yours. I blew it."

"Cool."

We shot for a while, back and forth, until Devin asked, "How do you use these things?" He was playing with the score pegs, which were strung out on wires crisscrossing the whole place, up above the tables, like a grid hovering over the whole room.

"Use 'em in billiards, I think."

"Oh," he whacked the wire above our table with his cue and it snapped, throwing the little round pegs all over us like confetti at a party.

"Devin!"

"Sorry,"—he was grinning calmly, chuckling—"I didn't mean to break it." I had to laugh too, and we started picking the pegs up off of our table and tossing them at different targets around the room.

"Well, anyway, no police." I was pleased, loosened up, having fun now.

"What? You mean from that goon yelling at us?" Devin was indignant.

"Yeah, I thought they'd be here by now and cartin' us away."

"Ah, I think it was only one of those dickhead parking attendants from the Golden Gate Theater. They think they're God on this block, or vigilantes or something. They're all assholes down there. Probably no one gives a shit about what happens to this place anymore—not enough to call the cops on us anyway."

We shot three or four more games before Devin got disgusted with losing. "Hey," I told him, "if you'd only pay attention and calm down a little bit you'd do a lot better. I'm only winning 'cause I play all week long up at the base—you know, there's nothing else to do in Fairfield." He nodded but gave me that look he always used to give me when he felt deserted somehow, like when I'd leave the bar or club we were in with a woman or something. And I've told him lots of times how stupid it is to romanticize that. It's no big thing to get a woman to go home with you, you only have to go out and do it to see there isn't any huge mystery to it. Obviously, Devin had ego problems. He was always rushing around, or drinking, or doing something crazy, always a little bit out in front of himself, trying to get someone to prove that they really cared about him by picking up the pieces after his more self-destructive experiments. But, you know, if there's one thing I've learned, it's that you can't depend on other people all the time—all they do is let you down. Via guiglielmo Marconi no. 81

Scene Two

Oh yeah, this one time we were all sitting in the Jack in the Box on Market Street in the heart of the Tenderloin at a little after midnight on a Sunday, after we'd drunk and talked ourselves hungry from an afternoon hangin' around 86 playing music. We were crowded into a booth, the four of us: Devin, Eric, Adrian, and I (this was when we'd first formed the band, before Lee had joined, and Eric had come by to hear what we were doing). We got our food and spread a lot of different burgers and a couple of orders of fries and some drinks out on the table. Each one of us started grabbing whichever burgers we thought sounded good and I spread a bag out flat on the table and poured all of the little bags of fries together onto it. Then I pushed the mound of fries into the center of the table and took some drink lids and filled one with ketchup and one with mustard and ketchup, which is what I like with my fries.

"Who wants one with everything?" Adrian asked, and I was about to say, "Send it down here," when this old guy sitting all alone in a booth over next to the windows on the Seventh Street side fell down dead right out of his seat.

I mean, there he was, huddled in his booth looking through the window suspiciously, watching the people walk by when, quietly, and without any fuss or anything, he just let go of himself and let it all fly out of him. He tilted first to one side, which is when I noticed him—and I thought it was only a drunk passing out—and his eyes were still open, gleaming under all the bright fast-food orange as he started going down, his body tumbling over out of his seat and into the aisle. He was limp and drifting for a second and then gained speed as he fell, coming down face first onto those cold and dirty tiles, his head rolling back and forth a couple of times after he'd hit the floor.

But the weird part was how absolutely absurd the whole thing seemed. I mean, nobody did anything about it for a while; everybody expected the guy to get up and stagger out into the street, or at least to climb back up onto his chair. But he was dead. He lay there, dead, and nobody knew what to do with him. Finally somebody went up and shook him, tried to feel for a pulse, and a kid from behind the counter came over and there was a lot of whispering and shit and oh, it was a big fucking deal now—like a war, or a movie or something, and everybody wanted to be in on it no matter how grisly and fucked-up it got.

So the manager appears, pushing his way through the civilians and ordering his teenage help around very seriously—of course by now they'd all come out from behind the counter to get an eyeful. Obviously this guy thought he was taking things firmly in hand, you know, showing grace under pressure and all that. An ambulance eventually comes: no lights on or sirens or anything. They cover the old guy up, put him in a body bag, on a stretcher, and then wheel him away—too fucking late.

We sat there in our booth eating our crappy food and watched the whole stupid scene unfold. We got pretty restless, finally, to get moving again, but Devin had to stay and see everything through to the end. Adrian and I started making jokes about it after a while, but Devin was still staring at the mob gathered around the corpse, and at the table where the old guy had been sitting. "I've never seen anyone actually dead before," he said. I guess it kind of amazed the guy.

After they got the body taken away we went back over to 86 'cause it was late and we couldn't think of anywhere else to go and had no money to go there anyway. Devin grabbed his pastels and a huge pad and started drawing the old man stretched out on the orange floor tiles with the looming windows of Seventh Street, and the Jack in the Box sign grinning over the whole scene, looking a little like Ronald Reagan. Devin usually stayed up on speed longer than the rest of us and he kept on drawing—not drinking anymore— while we split what was left of the bottle of gin we'd bought before practice and found spots around the room to more or less pass out.

When we woke up there was this pastel drawing on the wall of the three of us sleeping splayed out all over the place, as seen from

Devin's loft bed above. We all felt like hell and, in the picture, we pretty much looked like corpses.

"You gotta get it together, Devin," I told him, but he didn't crash until late the next afternoon, sleeping all through the day after that.

Scene Three

I'll tell ya, I ran into Rafael the other day. He used to live down the hall from Devin in one of the spaces at 86 Golden Gate. He's an old friend from way back. Sure, the guy's been into everything that's gone down on the S.F. art scene for a long time. He's lived at 86 for as long as I can remember. He kind of got all psychotic for a while there, about the same time I moved out and found a place with Maggie a little further up the hill, on O'Farrell Street. Rafael's folks came out from somewhere in the Midwest and dragged him off to an institution back where he was from. Devin told me about it—while he was in the hospital, I think. Then, a couple of months after that, good ol' Rafael just waltzed back into his old room and everything was the same, same as always.

Well, I ran into him down South of Market when I was walking to my car after visiting Annette at the Billboard Café where she works. He was probably on his way home to 86, heading up Seventh Street.

"Rafael," I said and he stopped—but it took him a second to recognize me. "Johnny Chan—you know, I lived with Devin for a while at 86."

"Yeah, Johnny. How've you been?"

"Okay, what's up with you?"

He looked away, a little strangely, and shrugged his shoulders. He was with this hardcore-looking dude who grinned like an idiot the whole time we were talking without saying anything. "So, how's Devin doing?" I asked, "I heard he was living with you since Eric had to throw him out."

"You know, I'm worried about Devin," Rafael said, which sounded familiar because everybody had been saying that for years, and especially since he'd been arrested and the police had beaten the crap out of him, and then the second time when he'd jumped off that rooftop because he didn't want to get beaten up again. "I mean, he's nice enough, but he can't seem to get it together."

"Yeah," I agreed. "God knows I'd like to help Devin, but what can I do? I should stop in sometime to see you guys."

"Oh, he's not staying with me." Rafael looked kind of strange again and said, "You know, Devin used to make a lot of fun of me, like I was weird or something." And all of the sudden he had this huge stupid grin, just like his friend. And his friend stopped grinning then and I could see him standing behind Rafael, looking down on him like he was worried. "But I'm an okay guy, aren't I?"

Of course I told him, "Sure, man, you were always okay by me." But it wasn't exactly true, because Rafael had taken a bunch of my records without asking me and had been carted off to the loony bin by his parents before I could get any of them back. "But where is Devin if he's not staying with you?"

"He's in jail, paying for his sins."

Which is, I guess, more or less true, because nobody's heard anything from Devin for a couple of months now. Rafael got all clench-fisted then, like he was ready to punch somebody, and sort of ecstatic too, I guess because he was imagining Devin in jail, but I don't remember what he said after that. I smiled a lot and said I'd come 'round and, well, see you later, Rafael, and I got the hell away from him. I mean, come on, I can't take those kinds of people anymore—they fucking scare me.

IV. ORIGINAL SOUNDTRACK RECORDING

Lyric from a song of Johnny's that Devin
wanted to use in his movie:

"If the sky should fall tomorrow
There's plenty left to do..."

8-9/1985
San Francisco

8: A CERTAINTY

I've spared you none of the telling details, I hope. A writer, I love the feel of my pen rolling across the paper, making out words with the certainty of black ink. Words are so comforting in the instant you read them, so necessary once they've been written.

Later I'll probably get up and walk somewhere: across town, to the park, through the Sunday streets of another country. After all this, it's still only the story of getting out of one's parents' house, of yanking the triangle into a line, of remembering without repeating, of trying to get to the moral of the story.

Maybe tomorrow I'll find something else to work on, although I have no words yet for the images, no thoughts for the characters, no feelings for the furniture. I'll be absolved by getting out of the apartment—especially the kitchen.

This is the last image—I'm holding it close—and it's of a woman. I'll be forced to open my eyes now; but I'll also have the certainty of the image to keep, another message to myself. Remembering it as something that's already happened but which I'd forgotten about; remembering it suddenly, involuntarily, like a déjà vu:

She's in a train car looking out the window—no, the window is open, gone, slid away behind the other pane, like in a Greyhound or a school bus. The wind, coming in through the open space, blows across our faces. Her eyes may be closed, as mine are now; she's only concentrating on feeling the wind on her face more closely. We don't have to be touching, but we aren't afraid to open the windows. Maybe the rushing air has made one of my eyes tear, because I feel it now rolling down the side of my face. Suddenly aware of the tickle, I realize that I must be awake. But my eyes are still closed. Only now they are becoming, the lids separating, bravely, no choice now, unavoidably, open to another day.

TESTAMENT OF FAITH

For M. P.

"I don't want to talk about that book,
I want to talk about my testament of faith."

—F. Scott Fitzgerald
in James Thurber's "Scott in Thorns"

I found myself in the uneasy confusion of being drunk and remember this:

I was dancing, pulling my weight up, then down, everything off-balance, circling around some woman but not touching her. I looked at Johnny, also on the dance floor, the trendy, neon paintings on the wall behind him, the other people in their black clothes jerking back and forth indifferent to one another, and I thought, I will have to turn sideways to get close enough to his ear to ask him, "What time is it?"

I did. I had to shout to be heard over the music: "What time is it?" I saw his skinny arm raise up, his neck bending and his eyes veered through the darkness, finding the watch around his wrist in the jangle of bracelets, chains, and black plastic rings and, "It's twelve," he said, screaming but calm.

The woman dancing in front of me let out a laugh, quick and percussive, like machine-gun fire. And I—something drastic now, please!—looked at her blankly, frankly puzzled. It was the first minute of a new day. We kept on moving recklessly to the music— she'd already informed me that she was going to take me home, that I was hers tonight. More people were coming out onto the dance floor, crowding us closer, and setting themselves in front of me like obstacles. She'd already stopped looking at me, stopped paying much attention to me at all, and I found myself watching the tight strip of bare stomach exposed behind her too-short T-shirt. From where I was her body seemed perfect—and she was acting as if it were perfect—so it must have been perfect. Who was I to argue with such certitude?

After claiming possession, she had contracted my fate with, "You can get out now if you want." How had I reacted to that? Had I smiled, or blushed? There were too many beers between my face and I to know for sure. Maybe I'd looked a little scared before, like I had wanted to get away.

Then my mind, pulsing strangely with every amplified chest-thumping downbeat of the Tears for Fears (or maybe it was Love and Rockets) song playing, the recently added sake chasing itself around in my head somewhere, tried to imagine making love to her.

Her T-shirt was black and I watched her breasts sliding around behind it, not quite playing peek-a-boo below the torn bottom edge— which was a credit to her breasts. Her teeth seemed to be grinning at me, like a shark, somewhere way out in front of her face. And I thought, "Okay, why the hell not? But let's get it the fuck over with so I can just pass out quietly somewhere."

Then the floor slipped, everything blurred and I could only feel myself, the earth seeming to shift beneath my feet. I grabbed the woman's arm to stay upright. I was in no condition to take care of myself, I decided, so I gave in to the inevitability of some sort of partnership. I was getting overdramatic: "She's my angel of destruction, beautiful, laughing now, and me sinking like this." But she only pushed me away. She'd already told me that she wasn't going to touch me until we got back to her place; this was some sort of rule of thumb of hers.

The music ended and began all over again as if nothing at all had changed.

I started—in an instant of sobering—making up excuses for actually wanting to go home with this stranger: "I can't help not giving a shit. I've got some things to work out. I've never really lived, have I? Loneliness sucks." Stuff like that. I mean, it was a kind of scary situation, or I was sure as hell going to try to make it into one. I already knew it would only be embarrassing and maybe boring being stuck with her the next morning, but, well, right then...

I don't remember why we left the dance floor. I was only meekly following the woman back toward the bar when your face— Melinda's face—appeared out of the crowd standing in front of the open windows.

"Mindy, hi!" I said over the woman's shoulder, wrestling my hand away from the stranger who had been leading me toward the bar, touching Melinda's arm to get her attention.

"Hi," she said, smiling, surprised to find me here. It was the first time I'd ever seen Mindy looking shy, or all dressed up for a nightclub.

I turned back toward the bar to figure out where the hell I was and the woman I'd been dancing with was leaning over to kiss some guy sitting up at the bar. I shrugged and shook my head in the wrong direction, toward the wall. The woman turned away from the kiss and came back to where she'd left me standing to tell me, "I've run into an old friend who's going to buy me a drink. I'll be right back." She pinched my butt, then forced her way back through the crowd and up to the bar and her "old friend."

"Mindy, you've got to help me get away from that woman."

"Her?"

"Yeah. No, never mind, I'm just kidding. I'll be okay. What's up with you?"

"What?" The music seemed even louder all of a sudden.

"How've you been?"

"I'm going away to Florence tomorrow."

"Really? Florence, Italy?"

"Yep."

"For how long?"

"Forever. Well, I'm only going to school there for a year, but I won't be coming back to San Francisco after that."

"That's a coincidence 'cause I've been planning to go to Europe myself in the spring."

"For what?"

"Just to live, change of pace and all that. To write. I've never been."

We were being silly now, laughing, and it was the first time I noticed how Melinda looked at me. She was acting like she'd meant to do something totally different but it had come out accidentally as a smile, and she did it more with her eyes than with her lips.

I remembered when we had taken our final exam in that statistics course at State, when she broke down and got all upset over how hard the test was and I'd put my arm around her and tried to calm her down—we had been the only two artistic types in that stupid G.E. course—and that had been the last time that I'd seen her, a little more than a year before this summer night in the sweat and cigarette smoke of the Nightbreak, that club out at the end of Haight Street, near the park.

"Are you going anywhere after this?" I asked and she shook her head. "Can we go somewhere? I mean, just to talk or something. It's weird, we were in that class together and I always liked you, but we never quite got to know each other, and now you're leaving."

She reached into her handbag, squinting through the darkness, shuffling things around. "You'll have to give me your address. I'd like to write, send you a postcard from Italy."

"You know," I had to lean down to say this, toward her head bent over the bag, which she'd set down on a table to make the searching easier, and raise my voice, trying hard to be heard over the music, my face practically in her hair. "You know," I said again, "I've had the biggest crush on you forever," and I guess it was true. It was one of those rare true thoughts that suddenly occur to you to say when you're drunk and later you think, "Wow, that *was* true, only I'd never thought it in exactly those words before that very moment." Sometimes other things come out, but this night I was lucky.

Melinda raised her head up, address book in hand, with that smile, and our faces were very close. "You," she made a little puzzled expression, blushed, and looked down, saying sweetly, "remind me of the first person I ever fell in love with."

"Oh, don't tell me that!"

"Well, you said something." She handed me the little book and I wrote my address and number in it.

Johnny came up behind me and I introduced them. Then Mindy's friends came over and we all went outside to the sidewalk. There was some talk about where to go—while I glanced back at the door, hoping that my dancing partner had forgotten all about me by now. At first Melinda was going to come with Johnny and I to a party we'd heard about at a new club that was opening down South of Market, but one of her friends needed to get some stuff she'd left back at Melinda's place, so Mindy suggested we take her car there, get the stuff, and then drop the friend off at her own house on the way to meeting up with Johnny at the party. So I waved good-bye to Johnny and followed Melinda and her friends away from the club, along the seedy remains of the '60s they call Haight Street, to Melinda's ancient black Mercedes station wagon parked at the corner.

The air outside was marine-layer cold and that made my head clear some, or I thought it was clearing, and I was thankful. Walking, however, was also making me aware of how really, really drunk I was, and I started worrying about saying or doing something stupid, or just falling down.

Pinto, Melinda's kitten, stood by the door, her head swinging to watch each of us pass by as we came into the apartment. She made especially big eyes at me, whom she'd never smelled before. I picked her up and held her against my chest. I sat down on the bed and began telling Pinto all about the evening so far, trying to concentrate on being coherent before I was left alone to make conversation with Melinda. I was looking hard into the kitten's eyes to keep the rolling walls from tipping me over, and she stared back at me with wonder.

Melinda and her two friends were changing out of their club-going clothes and searching here and there around the apartment for things in girlish flurries of noise and movement. I had the distinct impression of being on a ship in rough waters and that they were the crew scurrying about during a storm, battening down the hatches—except for Melinda's friend's boyfriend, the apparently wealthy passenger, who was sitting tired and bored in a corner waiting to leave. There was only the one room, a kitchen, and a bathroom somewhere off down a hall that connected all of the rooms together. Pinto crawled up onto my shoulders and lay down across the back of my neck and fell asleep. I found a gallon jug of purified water on the floor next to the bed and asked, "Can I drink about half of this?"

"Sure," Mindy said, passing by.

I tipped the jug and shook my head to clear it and then there were good-byes and Mindy's friends were gone and she came back into the room and laughed at me sitting on her bed with a kitten asleep across my shoulders like a stole and a jug of water in my lap.

"So, do you still want to go to this party that your friend's at?"

"What time is it?"

"'Round two, I think."

"No, not necessarily. I mean, it might be over by now. If you still want to go out we could try the Sub Club or something. That'll be going on for a couple more hours."

"No, that's okay."

"Good," I said, and our eyes acknowledged that we had only been acting polite and that we were each pleased to stay here together, and Mindy got out some candles. There was only a mattress, a stack of paintings, and some messy, half-filled boxes of packed-at-the-last-minute knick-knacks and housewares stacked against the walls. Almost everything she owned was already either given away or loaded into her car. Going through the kitchen earlier I'd seen that it had been completely cleaned out—and now the alcohol was making me hungry. We lit the candles and Mindy went off down the hall to get out of her makeup—I'd never seen her with makeup on before either, it occurred to me. What a strange social ritual, I thought: the nightclub.

"You know," I said to Pinto, "this never happens to me." Melinda came back in a nightgown. I felt something near my stomach tighten up when I saw her like that.

"I can't believe how lucky it was that you came along when you did. I think I might actually have gone home with that horrid woman."

"The one you were dancing with?"

"Yeah. I've never done that before, gone home with someone I didn't even know. She just came up, grabbed me and said, 'Okay, tonight: you.' I was so drunk. I guess I thought it might have been interesting maybe. Whatever. I only wanted to say that I'm glad I ran into you." I hugged her and she sat down next to me.

"Tell me about your novel," she said. "You told me once that you want to write a novel some day—so, what's it going to be about?"

I went into it as best I could and Melinda seemed impressed and then I asked her if I could see some of her paintings. She took a couple of her favorites out of the stack leaning against the wall and put them behind the candles so that we could look at them. The one that struck me the most, and I think was her favorite as well, was a self-portrait that showed her face looking out at you outlined by a dark hood, a bird's nest of twigs and bits of garbage below that—a tiny bird's skeleton cradled in the nest—and a poem at the bottom of the canvas that she'd written in first or second grade on that greenish paper ruled at about two inches with a dotted line down the middle.

"My mother sent me the poem and I had to make a picture out of it."

The poem read: "I see a nest in a tree. There is a baby bird in the nest. It is not happy."

There was another self-portrait in a frame laced with tiny fragile bird bones and tight white thread. "Bones," I said.

"I love bones."

"But what do they mean exactly, to you?"

"Well, they're structure," she said, not hesitating, "they're basic."

So we went on with our roundabout discussion of art and writing until Mindy surveyed the room, the still unsorted junk stacked against the walls, and said, "I don't think I'll be able to go tomorrow. I need a day off to relax before I go rushing off to Europe and leave San Francisco forever."

She got in under the blankets and I guzzled some more water, concentrating on staying present and aware. I took my clothes off carefully and slowly, trying not to trip over my pant legs, realizing when I stood up that I was still pretty drunk, although my head had seemed to clear while we'd been sitting there discoursing on art.

Melinda was lying on her back, looking up at nothing—or at something I didn't know about—and I got in under the blankets next to her. A gauze curtain that she'd tacked up over the room's only window, right above our heads, blew slowly across our faces with the wind. It tickled and we giggled about it. The air was a touch cooler outside and it felt good on my face. I was thinking that summer should have been over by then, but the nights were still relatively warm for San Francisco.

"Look over here." Mindy sat up, peering out the window, and I slid up beside her under the gauze shroud. We gazed out at Central Street, the dark green, cool and fresh-smelling Panhandle of Golden Gate Park off to our right across Fell. "Isn't this a great window?" We were on the second floor and I was looking at the row of Victorian houses across Central. Even though they all probably have the same floor plan and are set in a perfectly straight row, each one presents a slightly different façade to the street: the lovely, decorative illusion of individuality.

Melinda pushed the curtain back across the window and I slid my hand up her back. I watched her close her eyes and we pulled quickly together. It had been a pretty long time for me and, suddenly, here it was again. Then it occurred to me that it would be going away with Mindy, either today or the day after.

"I'm on my period."

"It doesn't matter to me if it doesn't matter to you."

"It doesn't matter to me. Anyway, it's light."

And later I let slip out, "I don't believe this—it's like our bodies were made to go together."

"You're saying a lot of things." I saw her frown in the cold blue light from the streetlight outside.

In an awkward moment I said, "You don't have to worry, I finished a long time ago."

"Well, it didn't finish for me."

"Good."

And then it was, "I've never made love for so long."

She looked at me with a worried expression. "You're kidding—neither have I," and we both laughed and her smile came back and we were different, closer now.

"Well, let's see how long we can keep it up." Finally, we got tired and stopped, not all at once—we just kind of drifted together into stillness.

She must have looked at her watch then, before we fell asleep, and said, "Now I'm definitely not leaving tomorrow. But I guess I'd already decided that."

Why am I writing such intimate things down? Whether it's good or bad writing is oddly immaterial to me here, I think. I seem to be seeking out the details, trying to remember the sights and sounds of our day and night together, Melinda. I want to hold your apartment and your room close in my mind, stretch the night I spent with you there out into an eternity, to see your face again, your pictures, to feel your presence here now as I write.

When Melinda had fallen asleep and the night gathered itself into an almost absolute silence, Pinto came up from our feet and made a nest in Mindy's hair. I couldn't go to sleep for fear of waking up and finding something gone. I was thinking about that and watching the light seep gradually into the room and humming a couple of lines from a song by the Smiths: "You should know / Time's tide will smother you..."

I liked the little scene we were making: Melinda sleeping in the glow of the streetlights, fluffy orange Pinto curled up in her hair. Then I couldn't keep my eyes open any longer. There was this weird feeling of things shifting and I woke up in the same position—as if no time had passed at all—but it was daylight outside. Leaning silently over her, I found the wristwatch that Mindy had left on her arm overnight and it said six a.m. She looked no different in the morning than she had the night before, not at all puffy or flushed. I lay for what seemed like a long time after that, drifting in and out of sleep, the morning breeze blowing in the window and over our faces.

There was an artsy black-and-white photo, a portrait of Melinda, pinned up on the wall to the right of the mattress. I didn't like looking at it; it was flat and dead somehow. I guess that's because photography never seemed to be a complete art to me. It's too exact, too real somehow, confining; and it's so much harder to find the artist in the work. But then there's Stieglitz, whose pictures are as good as any art I've ever seen, so I must be wrong. Later that day Mindy would tell me that she felt like a Georgia O'Keeffe waiting for an Alfred Stieglitz to come along and discover her. It's funny how you remember things not in the right order, but you always try to fill in the spaces and to arrange them until they make sense somehow. I suppose we're not sincere enough to recreate our memories exactly as they occur to us in our heads.

At some point Melinda got up to go to the bathroom or something, I must have been asleep, and she must have taken down the photo, I guess, because I found it filed away in the middle of the paintings leaning against the wall later that afternoon.

"There's no way I can stay in bed—I've still got like a million things to do." She slid herself around in the sheets and pulled the phone out from under the covers of the makeshift bed. "It's endless." She spoke to her cousin back East, telling her that she was going to arrive a day later than expected. I lay there feeling the breeze blow and the curtain sweeping across my face. The backs of my eyelids turned bright orange for a second as the sun came in, then deep purple with blinking yellow dots when the curtain got sucked back into the window frame. After the phone call, Mindy fell asleep again and I cuddled up close to her and Pinto.

There was this strange electric noise. It happened again and I realized that I must have fallen asleep as well. "Oh, that's my buzzer," Mindy said, surprised—she must have been lying there, like me, trying to figure out what was happening—and she went leaping out of bed and rushing over to buzz the downstairs door open.

She slipped her nightgown back on and, watching her, I remember wondering what it would be like to be a painter, your art limited to the visible. But no, even Melinda's self-portrait had had a poem in it. Here was an image though: Mindy's body sprinkled with freckles, her wavy reddish-brown hair stirred up by Pinto, short and fluffy on top, long in back, pulled behind her ears, her wide brown eyes looking at me now under the strawberry blond lashes, and the smile she kept aiming at me to say that everything was all right. The movement was important too, the way the nightgown fell in stages as she tugged at it and shook herself until it settled in place around her body. Maybe if you painted just the right instant in the motion it would all be there in the picture.

She stopped and leaned over and kissed me before letting her friend Julie in. Julie had come to collect Pinto. I heard them talking out in the hall and then Mindy brought her into the room and introduced us.

"I have to go out with Julie for a minute. It won't take long and I'll be right back, okay?"

"Sure."

As she got dressed to go out I talked with Julie, who was quite nice and good at making a naked man under a single sheet feel comfortable talking to a woman he's only just met. After they left, I drew a hot bath and laid myself into it. I heard Mindy come home again while I was still in the bathroom. "You splashed around so much." She giggled, smiling at me with her eyes closed, half under the sheet, hearing my footsteps on the carpet when I came back into the bedroom.

"I can't help it, I love water." She opened her eyes, still grinning. I kneeled down on the mattress and we kissed.

"Let's go out and get some breakfast."

"I'll take you to my favorite spot."

Dear Melinda,

I'm writing down our story to get it all clear to myself, to clarify the foggy images of the day and the night we spent together, the things I think I remember of you, of us. Sure, I could put faces on the thousand daydreams I might have of you today, but I can't write you a love letter because you've left me no address to mail it to.

I took you to Ming's Koffee Korner so that I could tie a memory of you to a specific, familiar place. I'm back here this morning, only a few weeks since you've left San Francisco, picturing you sitting on that stool over there, next to a different me, wearing your T-shirt with Winged Victory on it, the newspaper spread out on the counter, and you reading in the morning sunlight, which I remember quickly flattened into a blue-gray fog. I'm on the other side of the horseshoe counter now, across from where we sat that morning. I twirl my spoon around in the mug and watch the cream merging with the black coffee. I let the spoon rest on the rim, the whirlpool spinning 'round it, and pick up my pen to write some more.

I'd been awake and asleep so many times that morning that I had no conception of what time it'd gotten to be. We drove over to Ming's coffee shop at the corner of Leavenworth and Sutter and I kept kissing and touching Mindy, holding her hand in-between stoplights—when she didn't need her right hand in order to shift—and suddenly I was amazed by every mundane thing I saw, not so indifferent to everything as I'd been the day before. Even the colors of the day seemed new and strange to me; but maybe that was because I'd been so drunk the night before and had only slept in fits and starts.

When we came into the diner, Chinese Suzy grinned, nodding like she always does, looking over her glasses at me, and especially at Mindy, who she'd never seen with me before, saying, "Hi, hi, hi—good to see you."

"Good morning, Suzy."

"Two seats over here." She shooed us down one side of the counter to a spot near the corner, but under the high windows.

"Coffee first?"

"Please."

"Okay—sure, sure."

"She's so cute," Mindy told me.

"Yeah, I love it here—it's like a little piece of a '40s film noir left behind."

"Oh, I wanted to get a newspaper."

"I'll get it," I said, getting up.

Then, after we'd gotten our coffees and ordered breakfast, I asked her, "How serious are you about your art? I mean, do you plan on becoming a great artist, or is it only something to do for now, while you figure out what you're really going to do for the rest of your life?"

"No, I'm serious about it, but I don't push hard enough, I guess. I have a lot of ideas, but I should try to show more, to do more things. I feel like a Georgia O'Keeffe waiting for an Alfred Stieglitz to come along and discover me."

"I asked because I'm impressed with your work. You know, there's a lot of bad art around this town, but I think you're doing great stuff. Honestly."

"It's just hard to do it all the time."

"Yeah," I agreed, knowing how hard it is to write when most of the time there's only one thing to say. "Who was it? Some artist, when they asked him why he quit painting, he said, 'I got tired of filling in the spaces.'"

"Sounds like Duchamp. But I think he and all those Dada people were trying to say, you know, that life is art, or that we should live our lives the way artists do their work."

"Yeah, but life isn't art. I mean, if it were, why bother to do the art? People get confused, I think, because art comes so much out of our lives."

"That's true," she smiled at me, agreeing. "Still, sometimes the work is better if you leave the artistic process out of it altogether."

"I don't know. I don't think that's actually possible. Then it would be an accidental thing, like natural beauty or whatever. I mean, even just isolating a thing out of its ordinary setting is an important process of art."

"Oh, beauty!" she said and laughed.

I had to meet Johnny at the Soma Café near my house on Sumner Alley in SOMA at three that afternoon. Mindy drove me over there and we ordered more coffee, sat in a booth, and waited for Johnny to show up. He and I are in a band together and we had rehearsal that afternoon, so Melinda went home to pack the rest of her belongings into her car—she was driving to her parents' house in Connecticut before flying off to Europe from New York—and Johnny and I drove out to Hunters Point to rehearse.

It was no good at all. I was beginning to feel ill from the previous evening's drinking, and while we played I was thinking too much about Melinda's leaving. Our guitarist was nearly an hour late and we sat on the street in front of the studio on the blown-out and nearly deserted avenue in the city's most notorious neighborhood, waiting for him, watching the sky turn a deeper gray. The non-descript commercial building was also something of a shooting gallery and the people there made me nervous—I always thought we'd show up one day and all of our instruments would be gone. Then it started to rain and must have drizzled the whole time we were playing because the streets were wet and the air warm and humid when we came out, not like San Francisco at all.

Johnny brought me back to the Soma after rehearsal, where I'd arranged to meet Mindy at six. By then the sun had come out again and I was sweating from the humidity and the hangover that gets you in the afternoon with a kind of lost sleepiness and an empty-feeling stomach that you can't put anything into, instead of the kind that gets you in the morning with a headache and the runs. The world looked too bright and too clear to be real.

"So, what do you think of her?" I asked Johnny. "I can't believe I'm suddenly in love and everything."

"That's great. I'm happy for you. It's too bad she's leaving."

"Here she comes," I said, seeing her parking her car out the café windows. We watched her, locking the car door and crossing 12th Street. It's all open and bright here where the wide avenues, Van Ness and Market, meet and Mission Street curves to the left to become the main drag of its own neighborhood.

"Nice body," Johnny said, and I smirked.

Then Mindy and I were grinning, seeing each other again. We kissed and I went with her to the counter while she ordered.

Johnny came up behind us and said, "Well, I guess I'll leave you two alone."

"Okay, see you tomorrow maybe?"

"Yeah, sounds good. How about breakfast?"

"Call me in the morning."

"Okay, 'bye. Good-bye Mindy—it was nice to meet you."

She waved at him as he walked out and we went back to our table with her caffe latte.

"So," I said, looking at her all over again, "you still want to go see a movie, or what?"

"I'm sorry, but I haven't finished running all of the errands I need to run before I can go."

"That's all right, if I can come along with you."

"OK, sure, of course—I'd love to have you along."

"It'll be an adventure!"

We went to three of her friends' houses either to pick things up or to drop things off. I got to see the insides of all these different flats and to meet a bunch of new people, which helped to keep off the creeping sleepy sick feeling. While we were driving from place to place I checked out Mindy's cross-country itinerary and saw that she was going to be passing through where my parents had moved after retiring, and, east of there, where my grandparents lived. "Hey, why don't you take me along with you? We could stop at my parents' house, and then you could drop me off at my grandparents'. That way you'd have some company and we could split expenses." Mindy had been complaining, while saying good-bye to so many of her friends, that it was going to be a long, lonely trek across the U.S.A.

"Are you serious?"

"I'd have to quit my job without notice and then get another one when I get back."

"Why do you have to come back? I thought you were headed for Europe too. It *is* in that direction."

"Well, for one thing, I signed a year's lease where I live, and then there's all my stuff, which I'll have to store someplace. But it's mostly because I don't have enough money saved up yet to stay in Europe as long as I want to. The lease on our house runs out in March and by then I should have enough money to get set up somewhere, so that's when I've been planning on leaving. I thought I'd take all my stuff to my parents' house maybe, visit them, go see my grandparents, and then fly out of New York—since that's another place I've never been and have always wanted to see. Your itinerary is perfect, but the timing isn't so great."

"Well, we can write until March, and you can come see me in Italy. I'll be at the Cleveland Institute of Art."

The more out of it I became, the more jittery Melinda got with the anticipation of leaving; she was going on a long, exciting trip. Eventually she dropped me off at her place and went for a run.

Her room was empty now except for a pile of blankets under the bare window. I made a nest out of them in the corner and curled up. I thought back through all of the things that had happened to me since bumping into Melinda at the Nightbreak, smelled her all around me, and eventually drifted off to sleep.

The next thing I knew Mindy was calling up to me from the street below. I stuck my head out the window and she told me to buzz the downstairs door open. When she came in we were happy again—there having been a sort of uncomfortableness at our parting, our first moment of incompatibility—and I hugged her and asked, "Are you going to take me with you? I think it would be a blast to go on the road together, even if it's only for a week or two and it puts me behind schedule earning money for my Europe trip."

"I don't think so. You know," she held on to me so I would feel better about it and so I would really listen to her explain it, "when you travel with someone, you tend not to notice things." She led me down the hall and into the bathroom where she started the bath water running. "You don't interact with people. You get into a private little world, you and the person you're with. And I've already planned out this trip across the States by myself. But I think we will travel together. That's why we ran into each other at the Nightbreak last night and why we're both going to Europe. I think it's an omen. Until then we can write letters and get to know each other better. I write great letters."

I kept looking her in the eye because I did, after all, understand. She was leaving now and I was going to have to stay and wait for six more months before I could get to Europe myself. That was the way it was going to happen. It would have been stupid to change everything just because we'd accidentally run into each other in a club the night before she was set to leave.

"And you had better come over like you say you're gonna."

"Oh, I will—sometime after March." I paced around the apartment while she sat in the tub pouring water over herself with a bowl. I was trying to wake myself up, to clear my head, and so that Mindy wouldn't see that I was crying. It was inevitable now: I was going to lose her this evening. It was stupid to cry, though, because I was, effectively, happy.

I walked around the apartment singing another Smiths song out loud to tease Melinda, "Vivid and in your prime / You will leave me behind." It's funny how I was so hooked on this band then, and how now all of their songs seem to tell stories about me and that part of my life.

"You know," I yelled to her from the other room, "if you don't take me with you, I'll have to write a story about us—if only to kill time until I get to see you again."

"Oh," she said, coming into the living room and putting her damp arms around me, "relax. What shall we do for dinner? Are you hungry?"

We went to Chinatown to eat and there wasn't too much conversation. We were both looking around the restaurant a lot. Neither of us had ever been to this place before, and we'd chosen it for exactly that reason. We didn't need to say anything to each other anymore, but it would have been nice. I guess we were kind of exhausted.

I kept watching Melinda when she didn't know I was looking; I didn't want to be sitting there staring off into space, already imagining her gone and out of my life, or worse, trying to picture seeing her again in six months. There was plenty of that to come. I realized, even then, that I was happy—but without any excitement or thrill attached to the feeling. I was simply content. We seemed comfortable together now, with the kind of happiness you notice later, after someone's gone, after things have happened between you and you have no regrets, when everything goes okay.

Am I trying to make such pronouncements true by writing the story this way? Maybe we were uncomfortable and only killing time before we could each be alone and get on with our lives, this postscript encounter without any future having run its course. Or perhaps that's my paranoia and pessimism talking now. I want to ask you how you actually felt at dinner—about me, about us.

I'm talking directly to you again, Mindy, turning this story into a love letter. It's hard not to. I should have said all of these things to you that day we spent together or that night at the restaurant—but maybe I'm only figuring them out for myself now, or putting them into words for the first time here. Maybe I didn't say them because I know how useless words can be—and how important; because I want to do more than write to you, or about you. I don't want to turn this into a tragedy—it's just that there's a nothingness in the world that's impossible to avoid all the time and I fight its effects with my faith in words.

I'm walking home from work through Chinatown tonight, as usual, and sometimes, passing by, I glance in the windows of the place where we ate. Did I annoy you holding hands so much? I wanted to feel something finally touching me after such a long dismal period of loneliness and irony, even though I could already feel it moving away and leaving with you. The restaurant was almost empty that night, it being so late, and I didn't think you'd mind me touching you, and you didn't seem to.

I found a plaque across the street from the place, near the corner: It says that the first house ever built in Yerba Buena, the future San Francisco, was put up right there. So, you who believe in omens, would you say that's good for my faith in beginnings-again?

Missing you, I wonder what you're doing right this instant in Florence, as I sit here writing. Love becomes another question I don't think I'll have answered any time soon. I've finished the walk home from work and it's about midnight now—the first minute of a new day—and I'm sitting at my desk in the bay window of my room in my little house on Sumner Alley. All of my roommates are either out or quiet in their rooms. The drunks are all tucked up tight in the St. Vincent De Paul mission down at the corner and the dirty little backstreet outside, with its tenements and warehouses, is still and empty. There's a peace here sometimes, a stillness backdropped by the hum of the traffic around the corner surging along Folsom Street toward the freeway and the Bay Bridge.

There's only one event left to recount. If I raise my head up from the paper I can see the alley outside the window and the exact spot where you stopped your car to drop me off after dinner. It was about midnight then too. We hunted through your loaded-up station wagon for a souvenir, a suitable piece of clothing, something you said that smelled like you, that I could keep to remember you by until we were together again.

"So," I said, while you rummaged around in the back, "what are you going to do in Italy for six months without me?"

"I'll probably convert to Catholicism."

"It's a very aesthetic religion."

"And I want to have a big family. I want nine children."

Then, "Here," you said, "take this," and you handed me this blue rabbit's foot that was hanging from the zipper of your leather jacket—keeping the red and green ones for yourself—saying, "you'll need luck too."

6/1985
San Francisco

Printed in the United States
By Bookmasters